C.1

BILLY SURE

• KID ENTREPRENEUR •

AND THE BEST TEST

INVENTED BY **LUKE SHARPE**
DRAWINGS BY **GRAHAM ROSS**

Simon Spotlight

New York   London   Toronto   Sydney   New Delhi

SIMON SPOTLIGHT
An imprint of Simon & Schuster Children's Publishing Division
1230 Avenue of the Americas, New York, New York 10020
First Simon Spotlight paperback edition November 2015
Copyright © 2015 by Simon & Schuster, Inc. Text by Michael Teitelbaum.
Illustrations by Graham Ross. All rights reserved, including the right of
reproduction in whole or in part in any form.
SIMON SPOTLIGHT and colophon are registered trademarks of
Simon & Schuster, Inc.
For information about special discounts for bulk purchases, please contact
Simon & Schuster Special Sales at 1-866-506-1949 or business@simonandschuster.com.
Designed by Jay Colvin
The text of this book was set in Minya Nouvelle.
Manufactured in the United States of America 1015 FFG
10 9 8 7 6 5 4 3 2 1
ISBN 978-1-4814-4765-2 (hc)
ISBN 978-1-4814-4764-5 (pbk)
ISBN 978-1-4814-4766-9 (eBook)
Library of Congress Catalog Number 2014954732

Chapter One

Not-So-Sure Things, Inc.

I'M BILLY SURE. I'M TWELVE YEARS OLD AND I WOULD say that generally, I'm a pretty happy kid. I have a great family. I love my mom and dad, though I miss my mom—she's away a lot. My dad is great—a great painter, a great gardener—and a terrible cook. And even though my fourteen-year-old sister Emily can be a real . . . well, a real fourteen-year-old sister, lately we've been getting along pretty well. And then there's my dog, Philo. We're great buds, and he's a really cool dog.

I do all right in school, and I have friends.

My best friend, Manny Reyes, also happens to be my business partner. Okay, I know that having a business partner might sound weird for a twelve-year-old, but here's the deal (uh-oh, I'm starting to sound like Manny).

In addition to being a seventh grader at Fillmore Middle School, I'm an inventor. The company Manny and I run is called **SURE THINGS, INC.** We've had a number of successful inventions ever since we came out with our first product, the ALL BALL—a ball that changes into different sports balls with the touch of a button. It comes in two sizes. The large All Ball transforms from soccer ball to football to volleyball to basketball and even a bowling ball. And the small All Ball can change into a baseball, a tennis ball, a golf ball, a Ping-Pong ball, and a hockey puck. As soon as it came out, the All Ball was a **hit!**

At Sure Things, Inc., I do the inventing, and Manny handles the marketing, numbers, planning, selling, advertising, computers . . . basically, everything necessary to take my inventions and make them hits. We are a pretty terrific team. We've made some money, which goes back into the company as well as into our college funds, but mostly I invent things because I love inventing things. I also love working with Manny.

I even get to pick up Philo after school each day and bring him to work with me at Sure Things, Inc. Pretty cool. For me, every day is "Bring Your Dog to Work Day."

So, I repeat, I'm a pretty happy kid.

Except at this particular moment. Let me explain.

Sure Things, Inc. has just had to cancel an invention that we were certain was going to be our Next Big Thing. It was called the CAT-DOG TRANSLATOR, and it did exactly what it sounds like it would do. It took the barks and meows of pets and translated those sounds into human language. Sounds great, right? That's what Manny and I thought. But there was a problem.

The problem was not that the Cat-Dog Translator didn't work. Quite the opposite. The invention worked well. *Too* well.

Think about it. Your cat or dog sees you at your best, but also at your worst. You don't care how you look or how you're dressed or even what you do in front of your pet. Now imagine that your pet could share anything with the whole world, including the things you'd rather nobody ever knew. Get the picture? Well, this is exactly what happened.

This morning I, or rather, the Cat-Dog Translator, was the star of a school assembly during which I demonstrated the invention. At first things went pretty well—that is until Principal Gilamon thought it would be a good idea to bring his own dog in to try out the translator.

BIG MISTAKE! The dog blurted out to the entire school that Principal Gilamon farts in

his sleep—and while this was very funny, it was also *very* bad. Principal Gilamon was pretty angry. Make that very angry.

Other kids' pets revealed stuff about them that they were not too pleased about either. And so, by the end of the assembly, the big problems that came along with this invention were enough to make Manny and me decide not to move forward with it.

Which brings me to the whole "not such a happy kid at the moment" thing. Manny and I put a huge amount of time and work into developing the Cat-Dog Translator. We even got a sponsor to put up money to help with the costs of production and marketing, a big chunk of which we spent, figuring that the invention was a . . . well, a sure thing.

So we had to dip into our savings to give back the money we had spent. Our company, which got so successful so quickly, is now in danger of going out of business. And I'm not sure if I even want to invent anymore.

This afternoon Manny and I are sitting in the world headquarters of Sure Things, Inc., otherwise known as the garage at Manny's house, trying to figure out our next move.

"What about getting some money from a bank?" Manny suggests as he scans four websites at once, checking out short-term loans, interest rates, and a whole bunch of other money-type stuff I really don't understand. "Or, like I said earlier, we could invent something new."

"What if we just went back to being regular kids again?" I ask. "You know, like we were before the All Ball?" I feel a small sense of relief having said this aloud, after testing it out in my head about a hundred times.

Manny stays silent, his focus glued to his computer screen.

"I mean, what about that?" I continue, knowing that if I wait for Manny to speak when he's this locked in to something, I could be waiting all day. "No more double life trying to be both seventh graders and successful inventors and businesspeople. How bad would that be to just be students again? It doesn't mean I can't invent stuff for fun, like I used to do."

I pause, giving Manny another chance to respond. No such luck.

"For me, it would just mean that I wouldn't have to live with the pressure of always coming up with the Next Big Thing, of always having to worry about how much money my inventions are going to make."

Still nothing from Manny.

"You know my routine," I go on. "Get up, go to school, go home to pick up Philo, come here, invent, go home, do homework, go to bed, sleep invent. Then get up the next day and do the whole thing again. I mean, what if I didn't have to do that anymore? Would that be terrible?"

I finish. I have to admit these thoughts have bounced around my brain more than once on stressful nights trying to invent while also trying to complete homework assignments on time.

Just as I wonder if Manny is ever going to speak again, he turns from his screen.

"I'm sorry, did you say something?" he says, straight-faced.

"I–I–" I stammer in disbelief. Did I really just go through all that for nothing? Did I share my deepest doubts and worries with my best friend, when I just as easily could have told them to Philo for all the help I'd get?

Manny cracks up and punches me gently in the arm. "I heard you," he says, smiling. "It's just that things were getting a little too serious around here."

"Well, what do you think?" I ask. I really depend on Manny's advice. He's super smart and almost always knows what to do in a tense situation while remaining perfectly cool and composed. That is reason #744 why Manny is my best friend and business partner.

"You could stop being a professional inventor if you want," Manny begins in his usual calm voice. "But we both know that inventing is what you are best at. It seems to me that for you to be anything other than the WORLD-CLASS INVENTOR you are would be cheating yourself, and the world, of your talent."

Hmm . . . I hadn't really thought about it that way.

But Manny is just getting warmed up. "You're lucky," he continues. "You know what you love to do. You know what makes you happy. You know what you're best at. And you're only twelve. Some people go through their whole lives and never figure out what they are best at."

As usual, what Manny says makes great sense to me. I guess I am pretty lucky that I already know what I'm best at. I start to think about people going through their whole lives and not knowing. It's kinda sad. I feel bad for them. Ideas start to WHIZ around and BUZZ through my brain.

"It would be great if we could help those people," I say.

And then—*Ding! Ding! Ding!*—the light-bulb goes off for both of us. Manny and I look at each other and smile. The worry and indecision about my future dissolves in an instant.

"What if we invented something that would help people, whether they're kids or adults, know what they're best at?" I say, feeling energized by the idea. "I can see it now . . . a helmet or something that you put on your head that tells you what your best talent is. No more wondering what you're going to be when you grow up. With Sure Things, Inc.'s BEST TEST HELMET, you'll know what you should do for the rest of your life, the moment you put the invention on your head!"

Manny frowns.

Uh-oh, he doesn't like the idea.

"Well, the slogan could use some tweaking," he says in a mock-serious tone that instantly tells me he's kidding. "And we can just call it the BEST TEST. But . . . I LOVE IT!"

Leave it to Manny to snap me out of my funk and get me excited about a new invention. Now, of course, all I have to do is invent it!

Chapter Two

a Big Problem

THAT EVENING AT HOME I CAN'T STOP THINKING about the Best Test. It could just be the most important invention I've ever come up with. After all, most of the things I've invented—the ALL BALL, the SIBLING SILENCER, the STINK SPECTACULAR, DISAPPEARING REAPPEARING MAKEUP—make people's lives a little easier or a bit more fun. But this new idea could have a much bigger impact.

I start to imagine people who are struggling with what to do with their lives. They could use this invention and focus on something

that would make them really happy and maybe even help them make the world a better place at the same time.

I'm daydreaming about winning a big prize for my WORLD-CHANGING invention when all of a sudden I'm interrupted by someone at my door.

Knock-Knock!

Emily is standing at my open door. I look

up and see that she has a single braid dangling down the left side of her face. The braid is dyed bright purple. This is apparently the next "thing" Emily has decided to try.

For a while Emily was only wearing black. Then she moved out of that phase and began speaking with a British accent—all the time. Most recently, she started wearing glasses for no apparent reason. She doesn't need glasses, and the ones she had didn't have any lenses in them anyway.

Today, no more glasses, just a purple braid. I've learned that asking Emily "why" about any of these things provokes the same reaction as if I had accused her of making puppies cry, so I've gotten good at ignoring her latest "thing."

And actually, I'm surprised to see her standing in my doorway. She usually keeps her distance, and she almost never comes to my room. So I figure she either wants to: A) give me a hard time about something, or B) she's got a real problem she'd like some advice on.

"I heard about your assembly," she says, unable to hold back a little smile. "Really sorry I missed that."

All right, it's choice A. No big shock there.

"It was different," I say. "But it did show us that the Cat-Dog Translator wasn't really a good idea for Sure Things, Inc."

"So what are you going to do next?" she asks, sounding genuinely interested.

"We've got an idea that we think is really great," I say. "But I'd like to make sure I can invent it before I tell anyone about it."

Emily sighs. "Whatever," she says. "What I really want to know is what you're going to do about Principal Gilamon. You've been his GOLDEN BOY ever since the All Ball. Now, I'll bet you're on his official TROUBLEMAKER list."

Leave it to Emily to remind me of any potential upcoming disasters. Though she does make a good point. I've got to go back to school tomorrow and face

Principal Gilamon after revealing to the world that he farts in his sleep. I don't think I'm going to be his favorite person.

"Avoid him?" I reply, shrugging, knowing full well that is not going to work for very long.

"Good plan," says Emily, raising her eyebrows and running her fingers along her purple braid. Then she turns to head to her room. "Let me know how that works out for you."

Well, that wasn't so bad.

In the meantime I have got to get my homework done. I'll just have to deal with Principal Gilamon the next time I run into him.

"What do *you* think, Philo?" I say, leaning over and looking at him curled up in his soft bed. He stretches his front paws and moans: **"URRRRRRaaaa . . ."**

I kinda miss knowing what Philo is saying, but I do believe retiring the Cat-Dog Translator is for the best. Most of the time I can read Philo pretty well even without the device. And I do have one stored away in case I ever do need to know what Philo is trying to say.

. . .

The next day at school I walk quickly through the halls with my head down. My goal is to get everywhere as fast as possible and avoid seeing Principal Gilamon—or anyone else, for that matter.

No such luck.

Peter MacHale spots me on my way to lunch. Part of me thinks Peter MacHale must have a tracking device on me, because he *always* spots me first. He was the first one to congratulate me on the successes of the All Ball.

"Hey, Sure, when's your next assembly?" he calls out from down the hall. He cups his hands over his mouth and makes a very loud, very long, very realistic sounding fart noise. *PFFFFFT!* Everyone in the hallway is silent, but then I start to hear giggles.

"'Cause that was really fun!" Peter continues, giggling. "When Principal Gilamon—"

"When Principal Gilamon did what, Mr. MacHale?" booms a voice from behind me.

Uh-oh. I'd know that voice anywhere. It's

PRINCIPAL GILAMON! Not only is he about to see me, but also Peter had to remind him—and everyone else in the hallway—about what happened yesterday . . . not that he'd soon forget it.

"Uh, nothing, Principal Gilamon, I mean, I-um," Peter stammers. With that, he rushes down the hall.

"Hello, Billy," Principal Gilamon says coldly. "Any new inventions I should know about?"

"No, sir," I say. "I am sorry for what happened. I had no idea that my invention—"

"—would lead to students calling me Principal Gila-Fart behind my back?" he asks.

Are they really doing that? I wonder, but decide it's probably best not to ask.

"Because I've been told that charming nickname has been spreading around the school ever since the assembly," he explains.

I stare at my shoes, remaining quiet. What can I say that won't make things worse?

"I'm very disappointed in you," he says. "I thought you would be a shining example for everyone at the school. A role model. But now ..."

Briiiiiing!!!

It's the bell. The lunch bell. The *late* lunch bell.

"Well now, Billy, you're late for lunch," Principal Gilamon says.

Grrr! My stomach grumbles. I've never been late to anything (well, maybe Dad's dinner, but sometimes that's on purpose).

"Sorry, Principal Gilamon," I say, "I really should go—" I turn toward the cafeteria. Everyone is already in there, happily chewing away.

"We don't tolerate tardiness at Fillmore Middle School," Principal Gilamon says, looking at me. "I'm afraid I will have to give you detention."

"Detention?"

"Yes. You will report to detention on Friday and every Friday for the rest of the year until I say you can stop," Principal Gilamon says. "Now, hurry along."

I groan. Did Principal Gilamon just give me, like, a hundred detentions for being late to *lunch*? If it were a class, maybe I could understand, but LUNCH? Is the lunch lady with a hairnet going to give me an F in eating?

I would have never gotten detention for being late to lunch before. Oh no. Maybe Emily is right. Maybe there was something good about being Principal Gilamon's "golden boy" after all. I mean, I never asked to be his golden boy, but I have to admit, it was a nice perk. And now I have detention—every Friday!

• • •

After school I stop at home for a snack and to pick up Philo, who trots alongside my bike as I ride toward Manny's house.

I walk into the office. Philo flops down on his doggy bed. Manny is in the middle of a phone call. Just another day at Sure Things, Inc.

"Yes, it's called the Best Test," Manny says into the phone. "Well, why don't you wait and see what it does before you reject the idea. Great. I'll call you back when we have the prototype." Then he hangs up.

"Who was that?" I ask, settling into my work area, also known as my inventor's lab, or as Manny likes to call it, the MAD SCIEN-TIST division of Sure Things, Inc. In reality, it's just a corner of Manny's garage with a workbench, a tool cabinet, a parts cabinet . . . well, you get the picture.

"A counselor at State College," Manny replies. "The guy whose job it is to advise students on potential careers. I'm talking to him about getting some funding from the college for the Best Test. It will sure make his job easier. Either that or it'll replace him."

"You realize that I have no idea when the prototype will be ready," I say calmly. This is Manny's standard operating procedure—set up the investment, sales, and marketing side of things before my latest invention even exists. I'm kinda used to it by now, but sometimes I do find it a little overwhelming.

"As a matter of fact, I don't even have a rough sketch," I point out. "We only came up with the idea yesterday."

"Uh-huh," mumbles Manny, banging away at his laptop's keyboard, promising potential investors something I'll need to live up to, no doubt.

And I know what Manny's "uh-huh" means. It means: "You are pointing out the obvious, telling me things I already know."

I take a deep breath, grab a pencil and a sketch pad, and I start to lay out what the Best Test will look like when I finally do build it.

"I saw Principal Gilamon at school today," I say, hoping that maybe Manny has an idea to help me.

"Oh yeah? How was that?" he asks without looking up from his keyboard.

"Let's just say that at the moment, he's not my biggest fan," I say. Talk about pointing out the obvious. "Did you know that kids at school are calling him Principal Gila-Fart?"

Manny smiles. "No, but I like it," he says.

"Well, as you might guess, *he* doesn't like it," I say. "He even gave me detention every Friday for being late to lunch today!"

Manny gets quiet. I'm sure he's thinking the same thing I am: If I'm in detention every Friday, I can't invent every Friday. I start adding details to my rough sketch and compiling a list of materials I'll need to build the Best Test prototype.

A couple of minutes later Manny spins his chair around to face me. Philo lifts his head up at this movement, then places his chin back onto his paws.

"I got it!" Manny says enthusiastically.

"Got what?" I ask. "Another investor for the Best Test?"

"Not yet . . . working on it," he says. "No, I have the solution to your Principal Gila-Fart problem."

"Please don't call him that," I say. "It isn't helping anything."

"Okay, but this will," Manny goes on. "What if you started an INVENTORS CLUB for the kids at school? You could be the president of the club and help advise kids who join about how to make their ideas for inventions a reality. Principal Gilamon is always bugging you about being an inspiration to the other kids in the school, right? Well, this would fit right in with that."

"I don't know, Manny," I say. "You know I don't like being the center of attention. We tried the assembly, and look how that turned out."

"But this would put you right back on Principal Gilamon's good side," Manny points out. "You'd be a real hands-on inspiration to the other kids at school who have ideas for inventions. And you could probably run the club on Friday afternoons instead of going to detention."

"I have to think about this," I say, turning back to my sketch. The only sound in the office is the **clack, clack, clack** of Manny typing away.

As uncomfortable as the idea of being in the spotlight makes me, I have to admit, Manny's idea would solve a few problems. Not only would it help me with Principal Gilamon, but it could also help me tie together the two pieces of my life—being a seventh-grade student and being a famous inventor.

"Thanks, Manny," I say. "That's a really good idea. I'll go to Principal Gilamon's office tomorrow morning and see if he'll go for it."

Chapter Three

Inventing a Club

THE NEXT DAY, I ARRIVE AT SCHOOL BEFORE MOST OF the other students. Making my way to Principal Gilamon's office, I slip through the door and step up to the desk of Mr. Hairston, the principal's administrative assistant. I've dealt with Mr. Hairston a few times. He's very serious and he loves following the rules about as much as Manny loves sales figures—which means he loves them a lot.

"Good morning, Mr. Hairston," I begin. "I'd like to spea–"

"Number, please," Mr. Hairston says, holding

up his hand while not looking up from the work on his desk.

"Number?" I ask, puzzled.

"Do you have a number?" he asks.

"Um, no, actually," I say.

That does it. Mr. Hairston puts down his pencil and looks up at me. "Do you see that sign?" he asks, pointing to a sign on the wall across from his desk.

I glance over at the sign, which reads: PLEASE TAKE A NUMBER AND WAIT TO BE CALLED.

I look around.

"Um, Mr. Hairston, there's nobody else in the room," I point out.

"Young man, that is entirely beside the point," Mr. Hairston explains. "We have rules in this office, and as you can plainly read, the rules say that you must take a number and wait to be called."

"Okay," I say, reaching into a basket filled with plastic coins, each with a number written on it. My number is five.

"Have a seat, please," says Mr. Hairston.

27

Then he goes back to scribbling with his pencil.

After about five minutes, he looks up and calls out, "Number four."

I look around the room again. I'm still the only one here.

"Very well," he says, obviously annoyed that no one had number four. "Number five."

I get up, walk to the desk, and place my number five back in the basket.

"May I help you?" asks Mr. Hairston.

"Yes, I'd like to make an appointment to meet with Principal Gilamon after school today, please."

"In reference to what?" he asks.

"I'm interested in starting a school club," I say proudly, figuring that this will speed up the process. After all, it can't be every day that a student wants to start a new club at school.

"I see," says Mr. Hairston. He reaches into his desk, pulls out a form, and hands it to me. "This is form 4351-C, the School Club Start-Up form. Fill this out and return it by three fifteen." Then he turns his attention back to the pile of papers on his desk.

As I slip the form into my backpack and head to the door I hear Mr. Hairston call out: "NUMBER SIX!"

There's no one in the room but him.

As I hurry down the hall, I realize just how lucky I was to have been Principal Gilamon's golden boy. Everyone else who wanted to meet with Principal Gilamon had to go through Mr. "Take a Number" Hairston, like I just had to. As much as it bothered me that Principal Gilamon sought me out and acted like he was my pal—before the whole Principal Gila-Fart fiasco—being a celebrity had its advantages.

The school day itself is pretty uneventful.

FOR CELEBRITIES ONLY

Only three kids come up to me making fart noises. I'm feeling pretty good—except for the fact that I have to face Principal Gila-fart, I mean Gilamon, before I can get to the safety of the office.

At three fifteen I march back into Principal Gilamon's office and walk up to Mr. Hairston's desk. Being no fool, I reach into the basket to take a number.

Mr. Hairston looks up from his work.

"And exactly what do you think you're doing, young man?" he asks.

"Following the rules, Mr. Hairston," I say proudly, pointing at the sign on the wall.

"You already took a number—five, if I remember correctly. You are returning for your three fifteen appointment, correct?"

"Correct," I say, hoping that "correct" is the correct word for this situation.

"Then according to the rules, you don't need a number, do you?" Mr. Hairston asks. "Seeing as how you already have an appointment."

"Great," I say, tossing the plastic coin back

into the basket. "Can I just go into Principal Gilamon's office now?"

"I don't know, *can* you?" says Mr. Hairston. He looks at me. I look back at him. I'm not sure what I'm supposed to say. Finally, Mr. Hairston relents. "Fine. You may."

I turn and take one step toward Principal Gilamon's door.

"Provided, of course, that you have filled out the 4351-C form I gave you this morning."

I stop dead in my tracks. I forgot all about the form. Taking a seat, I pull the form and a pen from my backpack and start to fill it out. I'm about halfway done when the door to Principal Gilamon's office swings open.

The principal leans out and says, "Billy, come in, please."

I grab my backpack, my pen, and my half-filled-out form, and stand up. "I'll finish filling this out after my meeting, Mr. Hairston," I say, heading toward the open door. Mr. Hairston just shakes his head and goes back to his work.

"Sit down, Billy," Principal Gilamon says, closing the door.

I take a seat across the desk from him and wait while he settles into his chair.

"I think you know how disappointed I am in you, Billy," he says. "And not just because of your lunchtime tardiness yesterday. After the assembly, I got a few phone calls from concerned parents wondering what exactly we are doing here at Fillmore Middle School. Principals never like getting calls from concerned parents, Billy. NEVER."

I feel the knot in my stomach tighten with each word. Principal Gilamon is not making this any easier.

He pauses, takes a deep breath, and sighs deeply. "Now, what did you want to talk about?"

"Well, sir, I have an idea that I think will more than make up for the ... um ... the ... ah, problems with the Cat-Dog Translator," I begin. "I would like to start an inventors club here at Fillmore Middle School. I could be club president, if that's okay with you, and I would help students who join. I could guide them and show them how to make their ideas for inventions become a reality."

I pause for a few seconds to allow all this to sink in. Principal Gilamon remains silent, his hands clasped together on his desk.

"I know how you have wanted me to be an inspiration to the other kids in the school, sir," I continue, my mind racing for more stuff to say that might convince him that this is a good idea. "I think that this club might be a perfect way to do just that. And, um, if you wouldn't mind, the club could meet every Friday."

Principal Gilamon leans back in his chair and crosses his arms in front of him.

I hold my breath, waiting. If he hates this idea, the remainder of my career here at Fillmore Middle School could be a long, miserable slog.

Principal Gilamon leans forward, placing his elbows onto his desk.

"Billy," he says, a broad smile spreading across his face, "I think that is a TERRIFIC idea!" he says, extending his hand to me.

I'm so relieved that I let out a big sigh. Except my lip gets stuck on my teeth and it almost sounds like I'm making a fart noise. I look up at Principal Gilamon. Thankfully, he doesn't seem to have heard it. The last thing I need now is for him to think I'm making fun of him.

I shake his hand. "Thank you, sir," I say. "I appreciate this chance you are giving me. I won't let you down."

Principal Gilamon leads the way to the outer office.

"Mr. Hairston, please take care of the necessary paperwork to establish the Fillmore Middle School INVENTORS CLUB," Principal Gilamon says. "Well done, Billy. Well done!"

I have one foot out the door when I remember that I still haven't completed the club application form, which I pull from my backpack. "Oh, I haven't finished filling out this—"

"Never mind, Billy," says Principal Gilamon. "We're fast-tracking this project. Consider your application approved. Right, Mr. Hairston?"

"Yes, Principal Gilamon," Mr. Hairston replies through a tightly clenched jaw, staring at me like I have just committed a horrible crime.

Just before I leave the office, I toss the 4351-C application form into the trash.

CRIME: DID NOT COMPLETE FORM!

Chapter Four

Helmets and Hairdos

AFTER MY MEETING I HURRY HOME, GRAB PHILO, AND rush to the office. I'm happy that Manny's idea for an inventors club went over so well with Principal Gilamon, but I'm starting to get the feeling in my stomach that I always get when I have too much to do.

I can't even start to wrap my head around what's involved in running a club. And I haven't started building a prototype for the Best Test. I've got to make some progress on that today.

Bursting through the door to the office, I

see Manny talking on the phone while quickly scrolling through a website on his computer. It looks like he's shopping online.

"No, I don't think the Best Test will put your entire profession out of business," he says. "It can only tell you what you are best at. It can't read you mind, or put you in touch with dead relatives."

I can't wait to find out who *this* is.

Manny hangs up.

"What was that about?" I ask.

"That was the president of PSYCHICS AND MIND READERS OF AMERICA. She's worried that the Best Test will be so good at reading people's minds that it will make psychics obsolete," Manny explains.

"How did she even know that this is in the works?" I ask, amazed at how information somehow leaks out of this place.

"She's a psychic," Manny says. Then he smiles. "Seriously, haven't you checked our website lately?" He looks back at his computer.

"You put something up about an invention

I haven't even started working on yet?" I ask.

"All part of my greater marketing strategy," Manny explains.

"Aren't you worried that someone will steal our idea?"

We've had that happen before. A few months ago Sure Things, Inc.'s biggest rival, Alistair Swiped, pretended to be e-mailing as my mom in order to steal our ideas. Thankfully, Manny and I caught him, and we gave him a terrible idea to steal instead!

"Not this time," Manny says. "Our investors weren't happy with our decision to pull the Cat-Dog Translator, so I'm letting them know what we're working on. It'll bring their confidence up. You know, get the buzz going so they'll invest again."

"Uh-huh," I say. Now I just need to invent the actual thing. No pressure at all!

"So how'd it go with Principal Gilamon?" Manny asks. If I didn't know better, I'd say he was deliberately trying to change the subject.

"He loved the inventors club idea," I report.

"He's going to fast-track the club. We'll have meetings every Friday afternoon starting tomorrow."

Manny nods. He's happy his idea worked, but he's humble enough to not make a big deal about it. Reason #212 why Manny is my best friend.

Pulling out the list of materials I drew up the other day, I start piling stuff on my work-bench—a spaghetti colander, an old TV antenna, a handful of lightbulbs in different sizes and shapes, and a big bundle of wires, which I'll need to untangle before they'll be of any use to me. That's when I notice there's *way* more materials in my lab than before. Materials I'd never use—like old cell phone pieces, broken laptop keys, and . . . is that a RAINBOW WIG?

"What's all of this?" I say to Manny. His eyes are glued to his computer.

"Oh, that," Manny says distractedly. He types something on his keyboard and yells, "Yes!"

"Yes what?"

"I just won the auction!" Manny blurts. "Rare number twelve pancake-head metal screws!"

"Pancake-head metal screws?" I ask. "What are they? Why did you buy them?"

Manny twirls his fingers over his keyboard.

"For your lab!" he says. "So that you have more materials to work with. I want to make sure we get the highest quality materials at the most cost-effective prices. Successful products are made with quality materials. I read about it in my journals."

Manny is probably right, but I still don't know what I'm going to do with pancake-head metal screws. Or a rainbow wig.

After about an hour I have turned the colander into the helmet portion of the device, attached the lightbulbs to the sides and top, and screwed on the antenna. I place the helmet onto my head.

"How's it look?" I ask Manny.

He turns away from his desk and bursts into laughter.

"You look like a chef who's been kidnapped by aliens and is being made to reveal his secret recipe for spaghetti," Manny says.

"Great," I mumble. "Well, it's not how it looks that matters, but how it works."

"Okay, Best Test," I say, testing out its voice control commands, "I'm ready." The helmet begins to hum and the lights begin to flash.

A sudden puff of smoke comes from the helmet. If it were anything other than a Sure invention, I'd worry it's unsafe—this is definitely NOT something you should make at home. I yank the thing off of my head and start coughing.

"Well, if it doesn't work as a way to tell people what they're best at, we can always

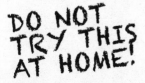
DO NOT TRY THIS AT HOME!

market it as an instant hair-styling device," Manny says.

"What do you mean?" I ask, waving my hand in front of my face to blow away the remaining smoke. I get up and walk over to a mirror. There, I see that my usually straight hair has been sizzled into curls. "Oh man," I moan. I'm used to early tests failing, but this is a whole other level. Maybe that spare rainbow wig isn't so useless after all.

"No, it's a good look for you, really," Manny says, unable to suppress another giggle.

"I'm going to call it quits for now," I say. "I'll work on this later. I still have homework to do and I've got to start thinking about the club. See you tomorrow."

"Yup," says Manny, without turning around. From the corner of my eye, I see him place a bid on a set of vintage mirrors.

As I pedal my bike home, with Philo happily trotting along beside me, I realize just how exhausted I am. But that doesn't stop the feeling in my stomach from returning. What do I know about running a club? Will anyone even show up? And if they do, will they have any good ideas for inventions? Or *any* ideas, for that matter?

After dinner I settle in at my desk to do some homework, but my mind wanders. I start thinking about my mom. I miss her every day, and sometimes I go weeks without hearing anything from her. I realize that this past couple of weeks has been one of those times.

I'm not getting anywhere with my homework anyway, so I decide to send Mom an e-mail. She moves around a lot in her job as a research scientist, and for reasons I don't really understand, she can never tell us exactly where in the world she is at any given time.

I write a long e-mail to her, filling her in on the failure of the Cat-Dog Translator, Sure Things, Inc.'s financial troubles, the idea for the Best Test, and the new inventors club. I'm not supposed to e-mail her about my ideas for new inventions, just in case they fall into the wrong hands, but I miss her. And she gives really good advice.

I hit send, take a quick shower to wash the curls and fried pieces out of my hair, and climb into bed. Finally, after a while, my thoughts calm down long enough for me to fall asleep.

I wake up the next morning feeling pretty alert. I must have gotten a good night's sleep. I don't recall waking up at all, which means that it's possible . . .

I jump from bed and hurry to my desk. Sitting there are fully-rendered blueprints for the Best Test! Yes! When I'm working hard on a project, sometimes I sleep-invent. I sleep-write

THE BEST TEST

blueprints for my inventions with my left hand. It's kind of like a SUPERPOWER, but if you asked me what's better, sleep-inventing or flying or being invisible, I'm not sure which I'd choose.

I look over the plans carefully, and they make perfect sense. I can even see what I need to do to make sure that no one else gets an unexpected hair-styling, or worse. After all, the first rule of inventing is BEING SAFE. #1 RULE

I start to feel excited. This just might work. This is going to be Sure Things, Inc.'s Next Big Thing. This will be the invention that gets us out of financial trouble!

My morning is off to a good start. I send a quick text to Manny, telling him that the blueprints for the Best Test are ready. Then I check my e-mail and it gets even better. Waiting for me is a reply from my mom. I eagerly open it.

Hi, honey, I'm so happy to hear from you! I'm sorry I've been out of touch, but I'm into a very intense phase of my research.

I'm sorry to hear about the Cat-Dog Translator. I thought for sure you had a winner with that one. But businesses have their ups and downs, and stuff happens when you least expect it. Hang in there.

Wow, the Best Test sounds fantastic. And I am so proud of you for stepping up and starting a club at school. You'll get to help other kids who, like you, love to invent. Well, work calls again, but I am so glad to hear from you. Love you lots!

Mom

Somehow, when I get an e-mail from Mom, everything else seems okay. I'm in a really good mood.

As usual, I speed through my morning, throw on some clothes, scarf down my breakfast, and run out the door so I'm not late for school. And because the first club meeting is today, I swing by the Sure Things, Inc. office to pick up a few things I'll need. Maybe Manny's online purchases will be useful after all.

Classes go pretty smoothly, but I can't shake this worried feeling about the club. Why does it seem like I'm about to walk into something I have no idea how to handle?

Never in my wildest dreams could I have imagined the sight that greets me when classes end and I arrive at the old science lab where the first meeting of the Fillmore Inventors Club is being held.

A crowd of twelve kids has gathered outside the room. This looks more like a meeting of the BILLY SURE FAN CLUB than of the Fillmore Middle School Inventors Club.

Every kid is wearing a Billy Sure T-shirt! But not just any Billy Sure T-shirt. This one has a horrible picture of me taken in the sixth grade.

It's the photo Principal Gilamon wanted to use on a poster, hoping to inspire kids just

after the All Ball came out. The poster has the words: *You'd Better Believe You're Gonna Achieve!* But the photo makes it appear like all I'm going to achieve is looking like the WORLD'S BIGGEST DORK.

Someone in the crowd spots me.

"Look! Here he comes!" shouts a boy who is not only wearing the Billy Sure T-shirt, but is also waving a copy of the poster, a copy I apparently autographed for him.

"We love you, Billy!" screams a girl who jumps up and down and points at me.

"We want to be great inventors like you, Billy!" calls out a boy holding up what looks like a robot missing its head, with one arm and two legs dangling from its body.

"Will you sign my T-shirt, Billy?" asks a short girl wearing an extra-large T-shirt that hangs down to her knees. I think her name is Samantha. She grabs the bottom of the shirt and stretches it out, hoping to give me a good spot to sign my name.

This is nuts! I mean, I know a bunch of

fan boys and fan girls who love comic books and movies and cool science-fiction stuff. I'm kinda one of them myself. But Billy Sure fan boys and girls? I have no idea how to deal with this. I hate being in the spotlight. That's why Manny always handles the press and publicity. I'll just have to try to change the focus from me to the other students and their inventions.

"Okay," I announce. "I want to thank you all for coming. Why don't we go into the room so the meeting can begin?"

I open the door, and the crowd of kids scrambles past me. I take a deep breath, then walk through the door to somehow start the first meeting of my brand-new club.

Chapter Five

Billy Sure Fans!

"OKAY, EVERYONE PLEASE FIND A SEAT," I SAY FROM behind the teacher's desk at the front of the classroom, realizing that I have never actually looked at a school classroom from the teacher's point of view before.

What I see is a bunch of kids all jockeying to sit in the front row.

"I want to be in front!" says the boy with the signed poster.

"No fair, I was here first and I want to be as close to Billy as possible!" says Samantha.

"It's okay," I say, wondering exactly how

teachers maintain control in a room filled with thirty screaming kids, when I can't seem to get a handle on the twelve in front of me. "Wherever you sit is fine."

The group finally settles into seats.

"I want to welcome you to the first meeting of the Fillmore Middle School Inventors Club."

A hand shoots up from the back of the room. I certainly didn't expect questions after uttering my first sentence.

"Yes?" I say, pointing to the boy whose hand is raised.

"I think we should change the name of the club to the BILLY SURE INVENTORS CLUB."

A low buzz of chatter spreads through the room.

"Actually, what we call the club is not the important thing," I explain.

"How about Billy Sure's Young Inventors?" a girl in the front suggests.

"I think the name is fine just as it is," I

say, wondering how long this will go on. "Let's start."

Another hand shoots up.

"Yes?" I say.

"Mr. Sure, can you fix my robot?" asks the kid with the broken toy.

"Well, first of all, please call me Billy," I say. "And maybe I can take a look at your robot after the meeting is over."

I have to get this meeting started, or we could be here all night!

I lift several boxes of parts and pieces I brought from my workshop onto the desk. I hope Manny doesn't mind how much stuff I took—but knowing Manny, he'll probably just purchase it all again anyway.

"I'd like each of you to come up, one at a time, in an orderly fashion, and take a couple of items from each box," I explain.

I've just barely completed that last sentence when everyone leaps from his or her seats at once and crowds around the desk.

Hands dig into the various boxes. Switches,

wires, metal parts, and unidentified plastic objects are all snatched up. Within a minute, the boxes are empty.

"Okay, now everyone pick a spot at the lab table and bring all the stuff you just picked with you," I say.

One by one the kids find a spot around a long slate lab table. It's got sinks, burners, empty jars, and beakers. The kids pile the pieces they took onto the table.

"Every time we meet, I'll ask you to bring your ideas in for inventions that I, and your fellow club members, will help you with," I explain. "But I thought for this first meeting, I would ask you to help me with an invention I've been having some trouble with."

Again a low buzz spreads through the room along with big smiles and wide eyes.

"We get to help *you?*" asks a girl wearing a baseball cap with the same terrible picture of me on the front. "This is like a dream come true!"

I bring out several bags of spinach, along

with beakers of flavorings, a few formulas I always use for food experiments, and a bunch of paper plates.

"Okay, club members—"

A hand shoots up, interrupting me. "Yes?" I asked.

"Can we call ourselves SURETTES instead of 'club members'?" asks Samantha.

"How about Billy Juniors?" suggests a boy.

"It doesn't really matter what we call ourselves," I explain, growing more and more impressed by the patience my teachers have when dealing with students. "What matters is that we all try our best to invent a way to make spinach taste good. I don't know about you guys, but I really, really, really don't like spinach and my dad is always making me eat it. I want to invent something that will take away the nasty taste of spinach if I'm forced to eat it. Maybe we could even find a way to make spinach taste like candy!"

A silence falls over the room that makes me nervous for a second. Then the whole club

breaks into applause. I can't help but smile.

"What a cool idea!"

"I hate spinach too! We're so alike!"

"This idea is better than the All Ball!"

People cheer. Then a kid in the back of the class raises his hand.

"But, Mr. Sure," he says in a timid voice, "you already invented the Stink Spectacular—the drink that smells terrible but tastes great! Wouldn't the formula for making spinach taste good be similar?"

It's a fair question. The Stink Spectacular is one of Sure Things, Inc.'s best inventions (at least, *I* think so). When I came up with the idea to make spinach and other gross food taste good, I wondered if I could use the same formula for the Stink Spectacular, too.

"The blueprints I came up with are only to make *liquids* taste good," I say. "It's the way that the particles are connected. When they're loose, like in liquids, I can make them taste good, but when they're closely packed in solids, like in spinach, I'm stumped."

There is a murmur around the room.

"So what if you freeze the Stink Spectacular and make it a solid?" asks the girl with the baseball cap.

"I really wouldn't recommend tasting that," I say.

The room explodes into chatter. Making spinach taste great—that could be the Next Big Thing!

"Okay, guys!" I say, raising both hands to get their attention. "This invention doesn't exist yet, and it's baffled me for a long time."

I walk around the lab table, plopping plates full of spinach in front of each student. "I want you to try out different flavorings and formulas to see if you can make spinach taste good. Now put on your thinking caps—"

"I've got mine on!" squeals the girl with the Billy Sure baseball cap.

"That's great," I say. "Okay, guys . . . ready . . . set . . . let's invent!"

The next half hour is filled with the sounds of liquid flavorings splashing and bubbling, edible powders being poured onto plates, and spinach being torn, cut, chopped, and smashed.

"I think I have something!" calls out one boy.

I hurry over to his spot and see a glob of spinach soaked with a pink liquid on the plate.

"I mixed this liquid with that powder, then heated the whole thing and poured it over the spinach," he explains. "Wanna taste it?"

I pick up a small piece of the pink, drippy spinach. Before I can bring it all the way to my mouth, it evaporates into thin air.

"Um . . . back to the drawing board," I say. "But good try."

"Taste mine!" shouts a girl on the other side of the lab table.

I walk over to her workspace and see steam coming off of a piece of spinach.

"I soaked the spinach in this stuff, then heated it," she explained.

I pick up the spinach and it instantly bursts into flames. I toss it into the nearby sink, where it sizzles and smokes.

"A little less heat, I think," I say.

"What about this?" calls out a boy at the far end of the table. He holds up a piece of spinach. It's as stiff as a board.

I take the piece and tap it against the hard granite table. It doesn't bend or break or shatter. It's as hard as a rock.

Briiiiiing!!!

The bell for the end of club period sounds.

"Okay, thank you all for coming," I say. "Good work. We'll continue with this at our next meeting."

As I help clean up, Samantha comes over and hands me a marker. She smiles at me. What can I do? I smile back and sign her T-shirt.

. . .

BiLLY
SuRE

58

That night, as I try to get a head start on my homework for the weekend, I start dozing at my desk. My head is just about to land on my keyboard when an e-mail arrives from Manny.

> Missing you, Buddy. How's the BT coming?
> M

BT? I wonder. Is that some kind of sandwich or something? It takes me a second to realize that Manny is referring to the Best Test, which, although I sleep-invented the plans, I have yet to build a working prototype for.

I shoot back a quick e-mail telling Manny that the plans are all set and that I'll dive into the prototype first thing tomorrow.

The next afternoon I'm at the office. It feels like I haven't been here for a week, even though I really only missed one day.

"Hey, it's my long lost partner," Manny says, actually turning away from his desk to look at me. "Sorry I couldn't be at your club. I had some calls to make. How'd the first meeting go?"

"You mean the Billy Sure Fan Club?" I reply. "'Cause that's sure what it felt like. They had these T-shirts with that terrible picture from the poster."

"The weird sixth grade picture?" Manny asks.

"Yeah, and one girl asked me to sign hers!" I explain.

Manny laughs, though I fail to see what's so funny.

"Ah, the life of a star," he quips. Then he turns back to his desk.

I get to work revising the helmet I put together the other day—the one that curled my hair. Hopefully the blueprints from my sleep-inventing will fix that little issue.

A couple of hours later I'm done. The base of the helmet is still the spaghetti colander, lightbulbs, and TV antenna, but I've also built in a mechanism that should print out what the test subject is best at on a piece of paper.

It gets late, and I have to be getting home. Philo needs to be fed, and I've got to eat. I slip the prototype into my backpack. Manny hardly notices me leave. He waves good-bye to me and immediately types on his computer. He bids on a set of deflated tires. What could *that* be for?

At home I pull the prototype from my bag. On the way to my room I pass Emily's open door. That's weird. She always keeps her door closed.

Emily looks up from her computer and glances my way.

"What is that weird thing?" she asks in her ever-supportive way.

"It's the prototype for Sure Things, Inc.'s latest invention," I say proudly. "The Best

Test. It can tell people what it is that they are best at in life."

"REALLY?" Emily asks. "Does it work?"

"I don't know," I reply. "I haven't tested it yet."

"Well, why don't you test it on me?" she says.

"Really?"

"Sure, why not?"

Fearing this moment of sibling generosity may pass quickly, I hurry into Emily's room for the inaugural test of Sure Things, Inc.'s Next Big Thing!

Chapter Six

The Best Test Is the Best

"THIS ISN'T GOING TO FRY MY BRAINS, IS IT?" Emily asks as I place the helmet onto her head.

"How could you tell if it did?" I shoot back.

"Ha-ha! Very funny, genius," says Emily. "Are you ready, or do we have to wait for a couple of hamsters to show up to run on a wheel to power this thing?"

"Let's find out," I say. "It's voice operated. Just say, 'I'm ready!'"

"I'm ready!" Emily shouts. Immediately a slow hum starts, growing louder and louder. The lights along the helmet start flashing in

sequence. Small sparks sizzle at the ends of the antennas.

"You okay?" I ask.

"Yup."

"Feel anything?"

"My head feels a little warm."

"All right, I'm going to turn the power up," I explain. "That should trigger the result."

Twisting a knob on the back of the helmet, the hum gets louder, the lights flash faster, and bigger sparks fly off the antennas. Uh-oh. This thing might be dangerous. I definitely wouldn't recommend trying it unsupervised. . . .

Ding-ding-ding-ding-ding!!!

When the bell stops ringing, the printer starts spewing out paper . . . and more paper . . . and more paper, until an entire ream of printer paper has covered the floor of Emily's room.

I stare at the paper closest to the helmet. It's blank. Following the long trail of paper, I step backward around Emily's room looking for something, anything written there. Still blank.

Finally, at the very end of the ribbon of paper is a single line of text. I read it aloud: "'Emily Sure is best at pointing out people's flaws.'"

Emily Sure is best at pointing out people's flaws.

I drop the paper and start laughing. "Well, I could have told you that without this invention!" I say.

"Just because I have deep insight into people is no reason to make fun of me," says Emily, doing her best not to crack up too. She looks around her room and sees the paper covering her floor. "Well, your invention may work as far as telling people what they are best at, but you definitely need to tweak the printout part. We don't need to use half a forest's worth of trees for each person."

"Excellent point," I say as I bend down and gather up the blizzard of paper in my arms.

"Still, it is accurate," Emily says. "For example, some of your flaws include being a know-it-all, always being messy,"—she gestures at the paper I'm gathering—"and, of course, not appreciating your sister's brilliance nearly enough."

"Uh-huh," I say when I have finally picked up all the paper. I feel like I'm holding a GIANT SNOWBALL in my arms. I stuff the paper into Emily's recycle bin. It barely fits.

Emily holds the Best Test, turning it to check it out from all sides. "I can't wait to take this to school!" she says.

Oh no! I snatch the device from Emily's hands. "You can't take this to school," I explain. "It's my only prototype, and I need to test it lots more, tweak it, and fine tune it before we can move into the manufacturing and marketing phases."

Emily ignores my comments and sighs.

"But . . . thanks for agreeing to be my first test subject."

"Hmph," is all she says. As I back out of her room I see one side of her mouth lifting into a small smile.

I hurry to my room where I shoot off a quick e-mail to Manny, telling him that the first test of the prototype was a success.

The next day I write to my mom.

I fill her in on the Best Test and the fact that Emily volunteered to be the first test subject. I know Mom always likes it when we get along. *Guess what Emily is best at?* I write. *Telling people their flaws! If that doesn't prove that my invention works, I don't know what will!*

Back at school on Monday I'm swarmed by the members of the inventors club, who are still wearing their Billy Sure shirts (I really hope they washed them) and eager to tell me about their progress.

"Hey, Billy, I covered my spinach in maple syrup!" says one boy. He holds up a plastic bag filled with a combo of dissolving green goo and sticky brown liquid.

"Uh, I would rethink that approach," I say.

"Billy, I put my spinach in the microwave for fifteen minutes!" says the girl with the Billy Sure cap.

The worst of all is Samantha.

"Hey, Billy! I can't figure out how to make spinach taste good, but I bought you these chocolates!" she screeches.

Oh man, all I want to do is get to class. But, still, these kids look up to me. I have to be encouraging. And they really are kind of sweet—just a little enthusiastic (okay, a lot enthusiastic). When I open Samantha's chocolates, I see there's a poem called "BiLLY MAKES MY HEART SiLLY!" tucked in there.

BiLLy makes my heart silly!
The way you invent stuff
makes my heart Fluff!
I love your hair!
And your nice eyes!
My heart is sure
about Billy SurE!

The rest of the day goes pretty well. A few kids that weren't at the first club meeting come up to me in the cafeteria and start to talk about their ideas for inventions. I suggest that they come to the next meeting. They say that they will.

That afternoon at the office, I unveil the fully-working Best Test prototype for Manny.

"Sweet!" he says, looking it over. "And, hey, if it doesn't work, we can always make SPAGHETTI!"

All right, maybe I should have seen that one coming, since the heart of the device is a colander. And I'm always happy when Manny is in a good mood.

"Very funny," I say, powering up the Best Test. "Let's see what you are best at, Mr. Spaghetti. Put it on your head."

Manny places the Best Test onto his head. "I'm ready, Best Test," he says. A loud whirring sound fills the office, followed by flashing and ringing.

And then the printer starts printing . . . and printing . . . and printing. Once again a huge ream of paper spews from the device.

"Gee, I must be good at a lot of things for the Best Test to need so much paper to list all of them!" Manny quips.

"Don't get too excited," I say, gathering up the endless paper. "The same thing happened when I tested it on Emily. My main task for today is to fix the printer part of the device." The Best Test stops. I wend my way to the end of all that paper and find a single sentence printed on the bottom. It reads: *Manny Reyes is best at math and computer science.*

"Well, it works!" Manny says, popping the Best Test off his head and handing it back to me. He looks around at the mountain of paper on the floor. That's my cue to start fixing the printer.

I find an adding machine—an old calculator that prints out numbers—in one of my boxes of goodies and pull out the printer section. Then I pull a roll of thin paper used for printing the fortunes on fortune cookies—seriously, what is Manny buying—and connect the two. After about half an hour, I'm ready to do another test.

"Who should we try it on next?" I ask.

"My parents are both home now," Manny points out. "Why don't we try it on them?"

I grab the device, and we head into Manny's house.

"Mom! Dad! Billy's here!" Manny shouts.

Watson, Manny's big gray cat, greets us, rubbing up against my legs and purring loudly. A few seconds later Manny's mom and dad meet us in the kitchen.

"IT'S THE GREAT INVENTOR!" booms Manny's dad. "What have you cooked up this time, Billy?"

"It's called the Best Test," Manny explains as I set up the device. "You put it on your head and it tells you what you are best at."

I finish making some adjustments to the helmet and hold it up. "Okay, who wants to go first?" I say.

"I will," says Manny's mom. "What do I have to do?"

"Just sit in this chair and I'll place the Best Test onto your head," I explain. "When you're ready, say 'I'm ready.' Don't worry. You won't feel a thing."

I place the helmet onto her head. The device hums to life. The printer starts buzzing, only this time a thin strip of paper comes out about two inches and stops. Looks like the printing problem is fixed! I tear the small strip of paper off and read:

"'Alma Reyes is best at keeping people's feet healthy.'"

Perfect! After all, she's a podiatrist.

"Wow, that's amazing!" she says as I take the helmet off her head. "I cannot stress enough the importance of removing dead skin, of scraping cuticles, and of regular foot maintenance."

"Mom!" Manny whines. "You know how that stuff grosses me out!"

"Your turn, Mr. Reyes," I say to Manny's dad.

I place the helmet onto his head. "I'm ready!" he announces. After a few moments of what has quickly become a smooth routine, the Best Test spits out another small strip of paper.

"'David Reyes is best at telling stories about the past,'" I read aloud.

"Remarkable!" exclaims Mr. Reyes.

I agree, since Mr. Reyes is a history teacher!

"That machine is right on target," Mr. Reyes continues. "Learning from the past may be the most important thing we can do to pave the way for a brighter future."

I had never thought about history that way. It's kinda fun. Manny, on the other hand, rolls his eyes and lifts the helmet from his dad's head.

I start to gather up the Best Test so we can head back to the office and wrap things up for the day.

"Thanks," I say.

"I'd say you boys have another winner on your hands," says Mr. Reyes. A big smile spreads across his broad face.

I'd have to agree.

Chapter Seven

The Club Meets again

I WAKE UP THE NEXT MORNING FEELING ENERGIZED.
I always get this way when a new prototype
is a success. It means that Manny can now
do what *he* does best and turn my idea into a
REALITY.

I check my computer and see that Mom
replied to my e-mail. This day keeps getting
better. I settle at my desk to read her response.

> Hi, honey, thanks for your wonderful
> e-mail. I am so thrilled that you and Emily
> are getting along and even more pleased

that she volunteered to be your first test subject! I'm laughing at how accurate your Best Test is, stating that what Emily is best at is telling people their flaws. Looks like you have another success on your hands, and I couldn't be more proud. I'm also curious. I'd love to try out the Best Test sometime! Gotta run. Love you lots.

Mom

Mom's e-mail gives me an idea. Maybe I'll bring the prototype to the next meeting of the inventors club. The kids in the club are all fans of my inventions. I think they'll get a kick out of having a SNEAK PEEK at Sure Things Inc.'s Next Big Thing. And it might be fun to find out what they are best at.

With the prototype up and running, the next few days are filled with marketing and production discussions at the office. In other words, Manny talks nonstop, showing me charts and spreadsheets, and I nod a lot.

Among the many things I've learned from the whole Sure Things, Inc. experience is just how important it is to trust your partner. Manny and I make such a good team, because we are each best at totally different things. He trusts that I can turn new ideas into actual inventions, and I trust that all those numbers, graphs, and projections actually mean something important.

The day of the second meeting of the Fillmore Middle School Inventors Club arrives. I pack the Best Test prototype into a large cardboard box that Manny got when his latest junk shipped, and label it PAPER TOWELS. I want to keep the prototype a secret until the meeting.

When the last bell rings, I grab the box and scoot to the science lab. This time everyone has taken a seat and is patiently waiting for me. I notice about five people who weren't at the first meeting. The club seems to be catching on, which makes me even more psyched about showing off the Best Test.

"Hi, everyone," I say. "I'm Billy Sure."

The room breaks into spontaneous applause. I thought maybe everyone had gotten over the whole Billy Sure fan club thing, but I guess not.

As the applause dies down, I place the paper towel box onto the desk in the front of the room. "I have something I think you'll all like," I announce. "I brought the prototype for Sure Things, Inc.'s latest invention to the club meeting today, and I'd like to share it with you."

"Did you invent a new kind of paper towel?" one boy asks.

"Can it absorb, like, a whole lake?" asks the girl in the Billy Sure baseball cap.

"Or maybe you've invented psychic paper towels that know when you're going to spill something and roll out to catch spills as they happen!" shouts a boy wearing a T-shirt with a picture of Thomas Edison with a lightbulb over his head.

This is getting out of hand.

"Actually," I say, "this is just the box I used

to carry the invention." I pull the Best Test prototype out of the box and set it on the desk.

"Is it a new way to make spaghetti?" shouts a girl from the back of the room.

Why did I have to use a colander? I think for the hundredth time.

"This is Sure Things, Inc.'s next invention—the Best Test," I say proudly. The room grows very quiet. "What this device does is tell you what you are best at. And, if I can get some volunteers, I'd like to try it out on some of you."

About half the people in the room raise their hands and shout: "Me! Pick me! TEST IT ON ME!" The other half slip their hands under their desks and look down, to be sure that they are not mistaken for someone volunteering.

I randomly pick three kids to try the Best Test. Okay, maybe not so random. I pick the first boy because he is one of the few kids in the class not wearing any Billy Sure apparel.

"What's your name?" I ask.

"Timothy," the boy replies.

"Now, sit right here, Timothy," I say, turning a chair around so it faces the rest of the class. I explain how it works and slip it onto his head. After a few seconds of the now-familiar whirring, humming, flashing, and ringing, a slip of paper prints out what he is best at.

"'Timothy Bu is best at counting steps,'" I read to the class. A murmur of laughter ripples through the room.

"That's true!" Timothy says as I take the helmet off his head. "I've taken four thousand, two hundred and fifty-six steps today."

"Thank you, Timothy," I say as he returns to his desk.

"Four thousand, two hundred and sixty-seven!" he calls out once he sits down.

It's now that I realize the Best Test is not

necessarily going to tell everyone what he or she should be doing for the rest of his or her life.

Next up is Samantha. I had to pick her, mostly because when I ask for volunteers, she waves her arms everywhere. She puts the helmet on and giggles. "I'm so, so, *sooooo* ready, new Billy Sure invention!" she squeals. A few seconds later the results come out.

"'Samantha Jenkins is best at watching TV.'"

"Wow!" she says, a big smile spreading across her face. "I can't wait to tell my mom!"

My third test subject is a sixth grader named Clayton. He's actually a random choice. His shirt is buttoned up to his neck and it's tucked tightly into his pants.

Clayton sits down and I slip the helmet onto his head. Out comes the paper:

"'Clayton Harris is best at going to the dentist,'" I read.

Clayton smiles. "I love going to the dentist. My dentist has the best purple lollipops, and I get a new toothbrush each time I go!" he crows.

"Well, I guess someone has to be the best at going to the dentist," I tell Clayton. I try to give him my most encouraging smile. Clayton smiles back up at me. And I can't help but notice that he really does have great teeth.

As I start to pack up the Best Test I hear a grunting sound out in the hall. Looking toward the door, I see two boys—I recognize them from the first club meeting—trying to squeeze a mattress through the doorway.

They finally manage to get it into the room and set it next to my desk.

"Sorry we're late," says one of the boys. "It took a while to get the mattress here."

"Um, what's it for?" I ask.

"We know that you do your best inventing in your sleep," says the other boy. "And since no one has had any luck inventing a way to make spinach taste good, we thought maybe you could fall asleep and invent it for us."

"That's not exactly how it works," I say. "You see, I—"

Cries of: "Please, Billy!" "Come on, Billy!" "Help us, Mr. Sure!" cut me off.

"All right," I say, trying to be open to what the club members want. "I'll give it a try."

I lie down on the mattress. Everyone in the club rushes to the front of the room, forming a circle around me. I close my eyes, but I'm not the least bit tired. It's the middle of the afternoon. Not only that, but THIRTY-FOUR EYEBALLS are staring at me. I open my eyes and they all lean in closer to see if I've solved the spinach problem. They don't really understand how the whole sleep-inventing thing works.

I close my eyes again and try to fall asleep, but after a few more minutes I realize how pointless this is. I get up.

"This is not going work," I say. "But thanks for your creativity. Why don't we go around the room and have people share some of their ideas for inventions?" I help the two boys move the mattress over to the side of the room. "Who wants to go first?"

"I do!" says a girl with long red hair. "I want to invent the INSTANT HOMEWORK COMPLETION ROBOT."

A buzz of agreement sweeps through the room.

"I love doing homework," says Clayton, and looks are exchanged.

"That's a nice idea," I say to the red-haired girl. "Who else?"

"I want to invent SPECIAL UNSQUEAKY SHOES that won't make any noise on the floors in my house. Then I won't wake up my little brother when I get up extra early to watch TV on the weekends."

"That one might be possible, but you could also just wear socks," I say. "Does anyone else—"

A knocking on the wooden doorframe cuts me off.

"Do you have room for one more?" says an all-too-familiar voice from the doorway.

"Emily!" I cry. "What are you doing here?" The high school is only just across the campus from the middle school, but most high schoolers never venture over here.

The kids all sit up straight and go silent at the sight of a high school student in a middle school classroom.

"I want to see what your club is all about," Emily says, stepping into the room.

"Everybody, this is my sister, Emily," I say.

Samantha's hand shoots up into the air.

"Uh, yes, Samantha?"

"Is Emily also an inventor?" she asks.

"As a matter of fact," Emily begins, stepping up to the front of the classroom, "I'm the vice president in charge of Next Big Thing development at Sure Things, Inc. I'm also pretty good at chemistry. I heard about your club project. And this afternoon I came up with a powder that will make spinach taste good."

A chorus of "Oooohs" sweeps through the room.

Emily opens her backpack. She pulls out a bag filled with spinach and a test tube with green powder inside.

Emily points to Samantha. "Will you come up and help me with this?"

That's my sister. Just walk in and take over the whole meeting, why don't you? But actually, I'm pretty curious to see what she's come up with.

Samantha joins Emily at the front of the room.

"Okay, now, Samantha, I'd like you to take a bite of this spinach," Emily says.

"But I hate spinach," Samantha whines.

"That's exactly the point," Emily says. "Go ahead, just a tiny taste."

Scrunching up her face and holding her nose, Samantha puts a tiny dab of spinach into her mouth.

"Yuck!" she cries. "Gross!"

"All right," says Emily. "Now I'll sprinkle a little of this SPINACH-ENHANCING POWDER onto another piece."

I don't love the name Spinach-Enhancing Powder, and it would never get past Manny, but I am intrigued.

Emily taps a few tiny green crystals from the test tube onto another piece of spinach, then hands it to Samantha, who pops it into her mouth.

Everyone, including Emily and me, leans forward, waiting for Samantha's verdict.

"It tastes a little better," she says. "Not great, but a little better."

Everyone in the room breaks into applause.

"Thanks, Emily," I say.

"No problem," she replies, slipping the spinach and the powder into her backpack. "That's just what we scientific geniuses do."

"Okay, meeting over," I announce. "I'll see everyone next week."

I have to say, the second meeting of the Fillmore Middle School Inventors Club was a rousing success.

As I pack up my stuff, I see the two boys who brought the mattress struggling to get it back out through the door. Maybe I should invent PERSONAL ROBOT MOVERS? I jot the idea down.

Chapter Eight

What Dad Is Best at

THAT NIGHT AT HOME I'M FEELING PRETTY GOOD. THE club seems to be a success. The Best Test prototype is working like a charm. And Emily was actually a great addition to the club meeting this afternoon.

After exchanging a few e-mails with Manny, I head downstairs for dinner.

Dad is hard at work in the kitchen, wearing his "Cooking is Art" apron and the silly, floppy chef's hat that Mom bought him years ago.

"Okay," Dad says proudly, lifting the cover

off a casserole he's just pulled from the oven. Steam rises from the bubbling dish. Steam that smells like a cross between boiled cabbage and the beach after high tide. "Who's ready for COD AND BRUSSELS SPROUTS SUPREME?"

Emily and I exchange a quick look, but we both remain silent.

Dad inhales the steam deeply. "Yum! Hand me your plates, guys."

We each hold out a plate onto which Dad spoons a big glop of his creation.

I move a forkful slowly toward my mouth, bracing myself for what is about to happen. The stuff tastes fishy and bitter and the sauce is greasy. I smile as I chew. Dad stares at me, wide-eyed, waiting for my review. I nod a bit too enthusiastically and make as close to a positive grunt as I can muster.

Now it's Emily's turn. She takes a teeny, tiny bite of the casserole, moving it around her mouth, trying to find a place on her tongue that might actually make the stuff taste good.

No such luck. I can see that she likes it as much as I do—which is to say not at all. But, as always, we don't want to hurt Dad's feelings.

"Very different, Dad," says Emily. "Surprisingly crunchy, which is kind of . . . new." I can just about see her brain plotting some emergency that would pull her away from having to eat another bite.

"That's my goal," Dad says, smiling. "Whether I'm painting or creating art in the kitchen, I bring a new point of view to whatever I'm working on."

I nod and put another, smaller bite into my mouth.

"Speaking of work," Dad says between shoveling forkfuls of casserole into his mouth, "how are things going at Sure Things, Inc., Billy?"

I fill Dad in on the Best Test, its invention, and recent success. Then it strikes me. I should try it out on him! How much fun would that be!

After dinner, Dad, Emily, and I sit in the living room. I slip the Best Test onto Dad's head. After its symphony of beeps, boops, bells, and flashing lights, it spits out the result.

I look down at the slip of paper and can't believe what I see written there. "'Bryan Sure is best at cooking,'" I read aloud.

BRYAN SURE is best at COOKING

Emily and I stare at each other in stunned silence.

"Well, well, well," says Dad. "I would've guessed that I was best at painting, but, of course, my artistic impulses can express themselves in many ways."

Neither Emily nor I want to be the first one to say anything, so neither of us says a word.

"I mean, I've always considered myself a great cook, but this now inspires me to bring my culinary art to a new level," Dad says, smiling. "And the timing couldn't be better! I just finished my latest series of paintings based on close-ups of Philo's tongue. I can use a little time to cleanse my artistic palette

by indulging in my other great creative skill—COOKING!"

I smile and nod. Next to me, Emily does the same.

"It's a win-win for everyone," Dad continues, his excitement building. "I get to take my culinary creativity to a whole new level, and you guys get to eat what I cook!"

Emily finally speaks. "A 'win-win' all right," she says, forcing a smile and raising her fist slightly into the air in a mock-triumphant gesture.

"So, did you guys test out Billy's invention on yourselves?" Dad asks.

"I tried it," says Emily. "It said that I was best at pointing out people's flaws."

Dad laughs. "Just remember, Emily, you're

good at lots of other things too. What about you, Billy?"

Up until now, I had never thought about trying the Best Test on myself. I know what I'm best at. After all, I'm the guy who invented the thing in the first place.

"I haven't," I say. "Maybe I will."

For the rest of the weekend, Dad is in his glory. He hardly leaves the kitchen.

For breakfast on Sunday, Dad whips up kale and cinnamon waffles, topped not with maple syrup, but with mustard!

"My creative juices are flowing now!" says Dad as he *thwaps* a glob of mustard onto his waffles.

And, of course, Emily and I have to stand up to this latest assault on our taste buds and stomachs without barfing or hurting Dad's feelings.

"I have to say that these are the greenest waffles I've ever had," I say with as much enthusiasm as I can muster.

"Aren't they?" Dad says proudly, shoving another chunk into his mouth.

For lunch that day Dad whips up a combination hot dog and hamburger. "I can't decide whether to call this a hot burger or a ham dog," he says.

It doesn't really matter to me what Dad calls it. I see him pull out a pack of hot dogs, a lump of ground beef, avocado paste, cottage cheese, and a blender, and my stomach starts to moan.

Dinner that night takes Dad's "creativity" to a whole new level. For starters, he combines mint chocolate chip ice cream with asparagus and then sprays whipped cream over the whole thing.

Words don't even come close to describing how GROSS this mess tastes.

Dad's cooking was always terrible, but now it seems that, spurred on by the results of the Best Test, his culinary choices have gone off the deep end. And there is something else troubling to me about this new development. For the first time, the Best Test was completely wrong. It took the thing that Dad is *worst* at and said it was the thing that he's *best* at.

I decide it's time. I have to administer the Best Test again, this time on someone who knows exactly what he is best at—me. I ask Emily to join me for the test, and so after dinner we sit in my room.

"This is kind of dumb," Emily says. "I mean, we both know what it's going to say. 'Billy Sure is best at inventing things.' On the other hand, here in your room we're safe from Dad's cooking."

"But that's just what's got me worried," I say. "If the Best Test can be so wrong about Dad, who's to say it can't be wrong about anyone else?"

I slip the helmet onto my head and turn it on. "I'm ready," I say, my voice a little shaky. A few seconds later the paper comes out.

Emily snatches it. Her mouth falls open wide and she starts HOWLING WITH LAUGHTER.

"What?" I ask. "What does it say?"

"Okay, okay," Emily says, trying to compose herself. "It says . . ." Again, Emily roars with laughter.

"Come on!" I shout.

"It says 'Billy Sure is best at spinach farming.'"

"Farmer Billy"

I sneer at my sister. "No it doesn't," I say, grabbing the paper from her hand. I look down and read aloud. "'Billy Sure is best at spinach farming.' What does that even mean?"

"It means you'd look good in overalls and a straw hat, holding a pitchfork," Emily says, bursting into a fit of laughter again.

"Very funny," I say. But not only is this not funny, it's really got me worried. Either my invention doesn't work, or I am really off base about what I'm best at. And Dad, well, there's no way he's best at cooking, right?

"You may think this is all one big joke, but it's not," I say. "This problem has to be solved before we move into mass production. I'm going to have to build another prototype to make sure everything is working properly."

"I still like the idea of BILLY THE FARMER," Emily says, getting up and heading to her room.

Later that night before I go to bed I shoot off another e-mail to Mom. I tell her about the not-so-great results of the Best Test, knowing that she, of all people, will get a kick out the idea of Dad being a great cook and me being a spinach farmer.

So much for things slowing down for me. I now know exactly what I'll be doing at the office tomorrow.

Chapter Nine

Best Test, Take Two

THE FOLLOWING MORNING I GET UP AND CHECK MY computer. As I had hoped, there's an e-mail reply from my mom waiting:

> Hi, honey, I laughed out loud when I read the results of your tests. We all know about your father's culinary skills, though nobody tries harder to be a good cook. And you as a spinach farmer? Spinach is your most hated food!
>
> But seriously, Billy, I hope there isn't a problem with your new invention. I know

how disappointed you were when the Cat-Dog Translator didn't work out like you'd planned. Good luck figuring this out. If anyone can, it's you! Gotta go! Love you lots,

Mom

I lean back in my chair. E-mail is great, and I love hearing from my mom, but it also reminds me of just how much I miss her.

But I don't have time to dwell on that . . . or anything, for that matter. As soon as I walk into school, I start running into members of the inventors club.

First, Timothy runs up to me.

"Hi, Billy!" he says. "Look what I invented all by myself!"

"Hi, Timothy," I say. "You know, now is not the best time. I have an exam, and the next meeting will be here before you—"

Ignoring me, Timothy shoves his invention into my face.

"It's my AUTOMATIC HAIR COMBER," he says proudly. "Watch!"

Timothy's invention is an electric tooth-brush with a plastic comb glued to the spot where the toothbrush normally goes. Timothy flips the switch to turn on his invention.

ZIP! ZIP! ZURRRR!

The toothbrush motor buzzes and whines, sending the comb around and around and around. Timothy lifts the contraption to his head. But his hair isn't automatically combed—instead, he knocks off his glasses and—**smack!**—pokes himself in the eye.

"Looks like it needs a little work," I say, doing my best, as always, to be kind. "Let's look at this at the next club meeting."

I only have a chance to take a couple more steps when Clayton catches up with me in the hall. I notice his shirt isn't buttoned up all the way to his neck anymore.

"Billy, look!" he says. "I made an invention. It's the SPINNING SANDWICH MAKER." He holds up a plastic spinner from a board game. Attached to the spinner are a bunch of metal spatulas. A different sandwich ingredient sits balanced on each spatula—bread, salami, cheese, lettuce, tomato, mustard, ketchup.

"Watch this!" Clayton says.

Just hearing those words makes me nervous.

Clayton spins the game spinner. The spatulas whirl around, sending the sandwich ingredients flying in every direction.

A piece of bread bounces off my head. A slice of salami slams into the wall and slides down, leaving a trail of grease behind it. Chunks of cheese land on the floor. And then . . . you guessed it, the mustard and ketchup sail through the air, splattering all over my shirt. A mixture of red and yellow glop trickles down, dripping onto my shoes.

"Um, I haven't figured out how to make the ingredients land together yet," Clayton admits. "Maybe we can work on that at the next meeting."

"Good idea, Clayton," I say, heading as quickly as I can toward my locker where I have an extra T-shirt for gym class.

After school I race home, pick up Philo, and ZOOM to the office. I have got to nail down another Best Test prototype.

I walk through the door and head to my workbench. Manny, who is on the phone and has his back to me, lifts his hand and wiggles his fingers to say hello.

"No, sir, I think *you're* confused," I hear Manny say. "This invention doesn't tell you what your dog is best at. Well, yes, we had been developing a dog-related device, but our focus has now shifted to learning what people are best at and—what's that? Well. I'm sure if your company invests in Sure Things, Inc.'s Best Test, what *you'll* be best at is counting the return on your investment. No, sir, I'm not trying to be funny. Thank you. I'll get that information right out to you."

"What was that all about?" I ask as I unroll my blueprints and start to gather the parts I'll need to construct another prototype.

"Oh, the usual," Manny replies. "Rounding up investors. Hey, how's the testing going?"

"I'm a little concerned," I explain. Even though it's been a day since I took the Best Test, I've been afraid to admit my result. In my head I practiced what to tell Manny. "I got a couple of weird results. The Best Test said that my dad was best at cooking and that I was best at spinach farming. So today I'm going to work up a new prototype and retest people I've already tried it on."

Manny cracks up. "The thought of you as a spinach farmer," he says. "I can just see you out in the field, in overalls and a—"

"If you say 'STRAW HAT' and 'PITCH-FORK' you may just have to find yourself another partner!" I say, cutting him off.

"Okay, okay, calm down, Spinach Farmer Billy," Manny says, still giggling. "I'd say a new prototype is probably a good idea. After all, I've tasted your dad's cooking."

"Agreed," I say.

"If everything is okay with the new prototype, then I think we can start production by the end of the month," Manny explains. Then he turns back to his desk. I think I hear him mumble something about spinach, but I choose to ignore it.

About an hour later I have assembled a second prototype for the Best Test. Building something a second time, especially when I have good blueprints right from the beginning, is generally a pretty quick process.

"Can we bother your parents again to test this new prototype?" I ask Manny.

"No bother," Manny replies. "You know they love seeing you."

I gather up the new device, and we head into Manny's house.

"It's nice to see you again, Billy," says

Manny's mom. "Is this another new invention you've brought over to show us?"

"Actually, it's an updated version of the Best Test," I explain. "Would you and Mr. Reyes mind if I tested it on each of you again?"

"Not at all!" Mr. Reyes booms in a deep voice. "Anything for science! Right, Manny?"

"Yeah, Dad, anything for science," Manny repeats in a tone that tells me that the sooner we head back to the office, the happier he'll be.

Manny's mom goes first. I put the new prototype on her head. A few seconds later it spits out the result: *Alma Reyes is best at keeping people's feet healthy.*

Same exact result as the first time.

Mr. Reyes goes next. Again, the result is the same as the first test: *David Reyes is best at telling stories about the past.*

"Seems to be working just fine," says Mr. Reyes.

While we're testing, I place the helmet onto Manny's head. His result is also the same: *Manny Reyes is best at math and computer science.*

I sigh as I pack up the prototype. I now know that the device works on the people whose result was correct the first time.

"Thanks, everyone," I say. "See you tomorrow, Manny."

I head for home to do the more serious and worrisome tests—the ones on Dad and on me.

At home I run into Emily first. She's in the kitchen, munching on a bag of chips.

"Are you still testing that thing?" Emily asks, spotting the prototype.

"Actually, this is a second prototype," I explain. "After the results for Dad and me, I got worried. Here, let me test it on you and see if the result is the same as the first time."

"Whatever," Emily says, lifting the bag and emptying the chip crumbs into her mouth.

I slip the Best Test onto her head. The result of the test is the same as the first time: *Emily Sure is best at pointing out people's flaws.*

"This is getting boring," Emily whines, lifting the helmet off her head.

"Hey, are you still testing that thing?" asks Dad, walking into the kitchen carrying a bag of groceries he just bought. "Wait until you see what I'm going to cook up for you guys tonight!"

He starts unpacking the bag. Out comes celery, a whole fish with its eyeballs still in place, a jar of hot sauce, and a bag of chocolate chips. My mind reels at the thought of the LATEST HORROR Dad is preparing to unleash on us at the dinner table tonight.

"Would you mind if I tried the Best Test on you again?" I ask.

"Why not?" Dad replies. "I'm sure you'll get the same result. I've never felt more creative or inspired in my cooking than I have in the last few days."

I slip the helmet onto Dad's head. *Here goes!* I think.

Just as with everyone else, the result with the second prototype are exactly the same as with the first one: *Bryan Sure is best at cooking.*

Oh no! I think. *What do I do now?*

"What about you, genius?" says Emily. "Try it on yourself."

This is it, I think. *The big one. Here goes . . .*

I place the Best Test onto my head. A few seconds later the result comes out. I read the piece of paper with great trepidation: *Billy Sure is best at spinach farming.*

I start to wonder if maybe it's time to give up on Sure Things, Inc. and the whole inventing thing and start a new life as a spinach farmer.

Maybe I wouldn't look so bad in overalls, after all.

Chapter Ten

Farmer Billy

THAT NIGHT I HAVE A HARD TIME FALLING ASLEEP. Should I really be a spinach farmer? I know I'm good at inventing things, so why didn't that come out when I used the Best Test on myself? And for the spinach farmer result to come up twice, on two different prototypes . . . that just plain scares me.

Could everything I've done with my life be wrong? How can that be? After all, I'm the guy who invented the device that told me that I shouldn't be an inventor. It doesn't make any sense at all, unless . . .

I don't even want to think about the possibility that the Best Test's basic design is faulty. Sure Things, Inc. simply can't afford two inventions in a row that never make it to the marketplace. No, I do not want to think about that.

When I finally doze off, I dream of fields filled with rows and rows of spinach. In the dream I'm wearing overalls, big boots, and the Best Test on my head as I walk through rows of spinach, yanking plants from the ground and tossing them into a big basket.

In the distance a tractor rumbles toward me, rolling right across the rows of spinach. I see that the tractor is crushing the delicate plants. Shredded green leaves fly everywhere.

At it gets closer I see that Manny is driving the tractor! Just as it is about to run me over, I wake up.

Well, that was really strange, I think as I climb from bed, anything but rested. Maybe I'm crazy, but I have to find out if the Best Test is right.

All week at school I have trouble concentrating. I feel like my entire future is on the line with the next decision I make. After school on Thursday, I decide the time has come to start my new life. If I'm really best at being a SPINACH FARMER, why fight it?

On my way to the office I stop into the local greenhouse. I remember being here with my mom when I was really little, but I've never actually bought anything here myself before today. It makes me feel kinda grown-up . . . and kinda weird at the same time.

The smell in this place is amazing with all the houseplants, veggies, and flowers. I take a deep breath. Maybe this really is what I was meant do.

I step up to the counter. "I'd like to buy some

spinach plants, please," I say to the clerk.

"Certainly," he replies. He places three six-packs of plants onto the counter.

Tiny green shoots poke out of the black soil. It's hard to believe that these little green things will one day grow up to be spinach and cause kids around the world to make excuses not to eat their dinners.

"Would you like the SAVOY, SEMI-SAVOY, or SMOOTH-LEAF?" the clerk asks.

Uh-oh, I didn't realize I'd have to choose a *type* of spinach. I didn't think this would be so hard. Then again, I'm supposed to be the best at this, or so the Best Test thinks, anyway.

"How about one of each?" I ask, smiling to hide the fact that I really have no idea what I'm doing when it comes to growing spinach. I pay for them and hurry from the greenhouse, hoping that that the clerk doesn't ask me any more questions that I can't answer.

I arrive at the office, plants in hand, resigned to tell Manny that I believe the time has come to start my new life as a farmer.

"What's up with those?" Manny asks, snatching up his laptop and heading toward my workbench. I can guess from what's on the screen that he's about to tell me all the things we need to do to get ready for the rollout of the Best Test. "You redecorating the office?"

"Manny, I've decided to follow the advice of the Best Test and become a spinach farmer," I say, trying to sound as serious as I can.

"Uh-huh," says Manny, plopping his laptop down in front of me. "So, back here on planet Earth, we have about a million tiny details to go through."

Speaking of planet Earth, I see Manny's bought a globe for his desk.

"Manny, I'm serious," I say.

Manny lowers his chin and raises his eyebrows. "Okay, first, that's the dumbest thing I've ever heard. And second, time is ticking away, partner. We've got packaging designs to develop, ad copy to refine, investors to make happy, retail chains to—"

"Why is it so dumb?" I ask, not willing to let go of this plan. "The Best Test has been way off twice now. It said that Dad was best at cooking, and I was best at, at . . ." I gesture to the plants sitting on my workbench. "At this!"

"I think 'inaccurate' is the operative word here," says Manny.

"Exactly," I say. "I mean, what if some kid uses the Best Test and it says that he's best at, oh, I don't know, knitting. So then he devotes his life to that, when really he should have studied to be a doctor."

"Knitting?" Manny shoots back, his eyebrows climbing even higher on his forehead. "Billy, knitting is a hobby, and maybe the kid *is* good at it, just like spinach farming can be your hobby. Maybe you're the best at spinach farming out of everyone else you know. But your job is INVENTING, and we've got work to do!"

I realize that trying to convince Manny is pointless, so I turn my attention to the charts and spreadsheets he's worked so hard to put together. As usual I understand about half of what Manny explains, but I trust that he knows what he's doing. A little while later I leave Manny to move full speed ahead on the launch of the Best Test, and head home with my plants.

After feeding Philo, I grab a snack in the

kitchen. I also place my new plants there in a sunny window just above the sink.

"Hey, look!" says Emily when she spots me watering them. "It's Farmer Bill!"

"Very funny," I say. "But I will grow these plants. And with your powder, they will even taste good when we eat them someday."

"Whatever you say, Spinach Boy," Emily says before heading to her room.

I finish watering the spinach and then go to my room. I sit at my computer to whip out another e-mail to Mom:

Hi, Mom, so you're not gonna believe this, but today I bought some spinach plants. I've got to find out if the Best Test is right about me. I'd hate to really have a secret ability to grow great spinach and not follow through on that. Speaking of the Best Test, I now have two prototypes. Were you serious about me sending you one? Let me know. Love you.

Billy

Mom's career has always been something of a mystery to me. I'd love to know what the Best Test says *she* is best at.

As I get into bed that night, my mind is racing. I can feel the stress of trying this new spinach project. I'm worried about letting Manny down. And I'm still wondering if actually releasing the Best Test is a good idea. I mean, I thought the Cat-Dog Translator was a great idea, and we all know how well that turned out.

The last thing that pops into my brain before I finally fall asleep is that tomorrow afternoon is the next meeting of the inventors club.

Just what I need—one more thing to worry about!

Chapter Eleven

The Return of Emily

THE NEXT MORNING I CHECK MY E-MAIL AND SEE that Mom replied.

> Hi, honey, I would love to try out the Best Test. I think we'd both really get a kick out of seeing what it says. When it arrives I'll let you know, and maybe we can set up a video chat, so it would almost be like we are together.

Mom goes on to give me an address in South America. I'm looking forward to seeing what the Best Test says Mom is best at. And I'm kinda excited about having a video chat with her. I have to be extra careful with sending inventions to Mom—again, I don't want any IMPOSTORS to steal my ideas—so when I ship the Best Test out, I ship it in a locked suitcase. I tell Mom that I'll give her the lock code on video chat so that only she can open it.

The school day drags. I fight to keep my eyes open as I move, zombielike, from class to class, all the time wondering how the latest

meeting of the inventors club will go. How can I inspire kids to follow their dreams when now I'm not even certain that *I'm* following my own dream?

After classes I arrive at the room for the meeting, imagining what might be coming next for me—president of the Fillmore Middle School Spinach Farmers Club, perhaps?

I am greeted by a noisy, excited bunch of kids. Luckily for me, many of them have brought in new inventions they have come up with or ones they'd been working on that they have tweaked since the last meeting.

"Hi, everyone," I begin. "Welcome to this meeting of the Fillmore Middle School Inventors Club. Who has something they'd like to share with the rest of the club?"

A whole bunch of hands shoot into the air.

"Me, me!"

"Pick me, Billy!"

"Ooh, ooh!"

I have to admit, the enthusiasm of the club members makes it easy to be the president.

Among the people with hands in the air I spot Clayton.

"Clayton, have you managed to work out the bugs in your Spinning Sandwich Maker?" I ask, pointing to him.

"Yes, sir," Clayton says, standing up quickly and hurrying up to the front of the room, carrying his invention out in front of him with two hands, staring at it to make sure it stays balanced.

"I call this the Spinning Sandwich Maker."

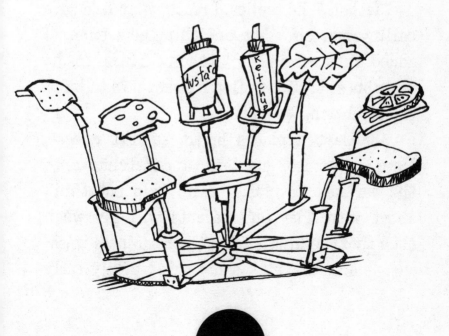

Clayton holds up his contraption for everyone to see. "You put the sandwich ingredients of your choice onto these spatulas. Then they are attached to a spinner I took off of my Climbers and Clingers board game. When you spin the spinner, the sandwich gets put together automatically."

Hoping to avoid another ketchupy, mustardy mess, I stop him.

"Um, Clayton, do you remember the problem you had the first time you showed this to me?"

"Yes, sir," he replies. I really wish he'd stop calling me "sir," but one thing at a time. "I added hinges from my kitchen cabinets to the spatulas so that they flop forward now to build the sandwich. WATCH!"

As Clayton places bread, salami, cheese, lettuce, tomato, mustard, and ketchup onto the various spatulas, I can't help but think about what Clayton's parents will say when they find the hinges from their cabinets missing. It actually makes me think of my early days as an inventor, when I would take apart everything from toasters to TVs to build my inventions. Maybe it's not so bad that Manny buys me supplies now.

"All ready, sir," says Clayton.

"Give it a spin," I say, taking a giant step away from the contraption.

Clayton spins the spinner. The spatulas whirl around and around. As they spin, each spatula flops forward on its hinge, placing in the center of the spinner, in precise order: a slice of bread, a dab of mustard, two slices of salami, two slices of cheese, a piece of lettuce, a slice of tomato, a blob of ketchup, and another piece of bread. A perfectly built sandwich!

The club bursts into applause! Clayton grins the biggest grin I've ever seen.

"Great job, Clayton!" I say as the applause dies down, realizing just how important this club is to some of the kids. Clayton heads back to his seat, getting patted on the back as he goes. It's obvious that he's found something he loves and someplace he belongs. Samantha is so impressed by his invention, she even offers him chocolate. It kinda makes all the worrying and lost sleep worth it.

"All right, who else wants to share their invention?" I ask.

"I do," says a voice from the doorway.

I look over and see Emily standing at the entrance to the room. "Emily?" I say, genuinely surprised to see her here again. "You know that club membership is only open to kids in middle school, right?"

Ignoring me completely, which is something else she's best at, Emily walks into the room. "Yeah, well, in a minute you're going to eat your words," she says, stepping up to a lab table. "As well as anything else you like, because I've been working on *my* Spinach-Enhancing Powder in the high school's chemistry lab, and I think it's a winner!"

I still don't like the name.

Emily opens her backpack and pulls out a bunch of containers filled with all kinds of gross foods. She opens a container and pulls out a piece of liver.

"Who here likes liver?" she asks.

"Yuck!"

"Ew!"

"Gross!"

Only one hand is raised—Clayton's. I have to give it to him—he knows what he likes.

Emily points to Samantha. "Samantha, right?" she says.

Samantha nods her head, smiling, clearly happy that Emily remembers her name.

"Do you like liver, Samantha?" Emily asks.

"No way!" Samantha says. "My mom likes to eat it, but I think it's really gross!"

"Perfect!" says Emily, placing the liver onto a paper plate and pulling out a small container. She sets the plate down in front of Samantha. "This is the latest version of my Spinach-Enhancing Powder. Let's see how it works on liver!"

Emily sprinkles a bit of the powder, now more a blue color than green, onto the liver.

"Go ahead, Samantha. Please take a bite."

Scrunching up her face, bracing herself for the worst, Samantha pops a piece of liver into the mouth. Her face starts to relax, then her eyes open wide. "IT TASTES GREAT!" she cries. "How did you do that?"

Emily smiles. "Okay, who hates lima beans?" she asks, opening the next food container.

Everyone raises a hand . . . even Clayton.

"Okay, and what's your name?" Emily asks, pointing to a boy in the back of the room.

"Robert," he replies.

"All right, Robert, try this," she says, sprinkling some of her powder onto a small pile of lima beans.

Once again Emily has waltzed in to my club and taken over. But I'm glad. The kids in the club really seem to be getting a kick out her being here. And, if this powder of hers works as well as she says . . . well, one step at a time.

Robert picks up a lima bean and looks at it as if it were radioactive.

"Go ahead," Emily encourages him.

He eats the bean. "Wow!" he says. "This tastes better than candy!"

"Okay, I've saved the best for last," she says, placing some spinach onto a plate. "And Billy, I think you should taste this sample."

She sprinkles some of the powder onto the spinach. It disappears into the folds of the leaves. I catch myself wondering which variety of spinach this might be.

I shove the spinach into my mouth and chew. The entire club leans toward me, waiting to see my reaction. The spinach has a slightly sweet, slightly salty flavor that actually tastes great. It tastes better than before with the Spinach-Enhancing Powder.

"Fantastic!" I say as the room breaks into applause. "And it seems to work on anything."

My mind starts racing, going through a bunch of things all at once. First, I realize that Emily and I might be more similar than we thought—or more than she will ever admit.

Second, maybe the Best Test isn't the greatest idea after all. In reality, maybe it's Emily who's come up with the better invention.

And third, with some fine tuning, Emily's powder could actually turn out to be Sure Things, Inc.'s Next Big Thing!

Briiiiiiing!!!

The bell sounds, interrupting my thoughts and signaling that the meeting is over.

"Thank you all for coming," I say. "I'll see you next week." I turn to Emily.

"Would you maybe come to the Sure Things, Inc. office right now so we can fine tune your powder?" I ask. "I think you may really have something there."

"Okay," Emily says. "But I need a promotion. I'm a vice president now. I'm thinking something along the lines of inventor-in-chief."

Chapter Twelve

Gross to Good!

EMILY CARRIES PHILO OVER TO THE OFFICE IN her arms. I don't tell her that he likes to trot by me—she's too busy petting him, saying things like, "We need to invent some nicer smelling shampoo for you," while simultaneously saying, "You're the best dog in the world!"

"Check out my workbench," I say once we're at the office, "or as we like to call it—the mad scientist division of Sure Things Inc."

Emily walks over to the piles of wires, switches, and tools that cover my workbench.

I notice that Manny's added two mini pitchforks.

"When's the last time you actually saw the surface of the workbench?" Emily asks.

"Probably the day we opened the office," I say.

She looks over at my cabinets, shelves, and peg boards, then pulls open a drawer labeled SMALL SWITCHES, in which she sees a bunch of tiny lightbulbs—and the rainbow wig. "What's up with this?" she asks.

"WHAT'S UP WITH WHAT?" I reply casually.

"So what have you got for us, Emily?" Manny asks, anxious to get on with the business at hand.

She plops her backpack right down into the middle of my workbench, sending parts and tools flying in every direction. Then she unzips it, pulling out a container of her powder and a chemical formula written on a note card.

Now we're getting somewhere. Manny and I look over Emily's shoulder at the formula. It's pretty complex. Sometimes I forget just how smart Emily is.

"That's interesting," Manny says, pointing to a list of ingredients that must be mixed in precise order.

"Hmm . . . ," Manny says. "Have you considered switching the order of these two steps?" he asks, pointing to the paper.

"Interesting," says Emily, intrigued by Manny's question. "I never thought of that, but I can see that making that change might help the rest of these combine more quickly."

"Which should increase the range of food that the powder works on," adds Manny. "It just works on liver, lima beans, and spinach now, right? If we can tweak this formula to work on any food, we may just have a huge hit on our hands."

"Let's try it," I suggest, pulling out a plastic bin and sweeping the debris—otherwise known as my work—from the workbench to give Emily room to play with her formula.

"While you're doing that," Manny says to

Emily, "I'll run into my house and grab the worst-tasting food I can find."

A short while later Emily finishes reworking her formula. The powder that started as green, then morphed to blue, is now plain white. If you didn't know any better, you'd think that you were just sprinkling salt on your food.

Manny places platefuls of Brussels sprouts, horseradish, and chocolate chips on the workbench. "I'm curious," he says, "what the powder will do to food that already tastes good. Well, go ahead," he says, this time looking at Emily. "You're the inventor. You do the honors."

She sprinkles the powder onto all of the food. I pop a Brussels sprout into my mouth.

KERRRR-POW!

A taste unlike anything I've ever experienced explodes onto my taste buds. I can't even describe it or compare it to any other food. It just tastes *fantastic!*

"This Brussels sprout is the best thing I've ever tasted," I say.

Manny picks up a small dab of horseradish.

Normally even a tiny taste can cause him to choke and tear up. Manny eats it, then grabs more.

"Amazing!" he says.

Finally, we grab handfuls of chocolate chips and each eat some. We all look at each other and smile.

"It's like all the goodness of chocolate, times a million!" Emily cries.

"This is fantastic!" I say, starting to feel better about my doubts with the Best Test. Having a great backup product always makes abandoning the first idea much easier to swallow—so to speak. "This could be a hit for Sure Things, Inc. After all, Emily is a Sure," I say, mostly to Manny.

"I agree," Manny says. I can see the wheels spinning in his brain just from the expression on his face. "But we need to field test it with a bigger sample group before we can think about making it one of our products."

That's when it hits me.

"I've got it!" I announce. "What if we tested

it on the pickiest eaters in the world—middle school kids?!"

"You mean, see if we can make even cafeteria food taste good?" asks Emily.

"We should try it with food that's even more disgusting," I say. "What if Dad cooks a special dinner as a fund-raiser for the inventors club? Principal Gilamon is always encouraging parents to get more involved in school activities. We can invite everyone in the school to try out our new product. Dad will think we're celebrating his great cooking. But we'll make sure to sprinkle a little powder on all the food before the kids eat it—without him knowing of course. If the kids like the food, he'll feel great, and we'll know that powder works on anything!"

"Let's do it!" says Manny, returning to his desk to start working on a marketing plan for Emily's powder, though I see him check the auction website in a new tab.

At dinner that night, Dad serves up something he calls beet surprise.

"What's the surprise?" Emily asks.

"The surprise," Dad says, "is that the beets are stuffed with more beets!"

"Great," Emily says. Then as Dad heads back to the kitchen, she leans over and whispers to me, "I *hate* beets!"

Before Dad returns, Emily sprinkles a little of her powder on each of our servings.

"Well, dig in!" says Dad, joining us at the table.

I cut into my beet, discover the beet stuffing, and munch on a forkful.

KERRRR-POW!

"Wow, this is really delicious," I say. And, thanks to Emily's powder, I'm telling the truth.

"So, Dad, I had an idea about how you could get more people to sample your cooking," I say.

"I'm all ears," Dad says. "Which reminds me. I should pick up some corn—I have a corn and blue cheese soup recipe that I've been dying to try out."

"Mmhmm. So anyway, we're thinking of holding a fund-raiser for the inventors club. How would you like to come out and cook

dinner for everyone?" I ask. "You plan the menu. You cook the food. And Emily, Manny, and I will help serve."

"*FANTASTIC!*" Dad says. "I'll start planning the menu tonight!"

As I help Dad clean up after dinner, I notice that my spinach plants are thriving. They are twice as big as when I bought them. Hmmm, maybe I really am good at growing spinach. But that doesn't mean that I'm not good at inventing. My enthusiasm for the Best Test is fading the more I think about it.

Manny advertises the fund-raiser dinner so much, we have enough kids to fill the entire cafeteria on the evening of the event! I'm really excited to try Emily's product out on the pickiest eaters.

Dad arrives after school and Emily walks over from the high school. He made all of the food at home because the kitchen can only be used by cafeteria staff. Apparently they're really picky about that. Who knew?

"Can you grab that?" he asks, pointing to a large cooler in the back of his car.

I carry the cooler, Manny takes a tray of food, and Emily picks up a case of juice. We bring everything into the cafeteria.

As each delicacy is unwrapped, Emily, Manny, and I take it and place it out where the kids can help themselves—but not before sprinkling each dish with some of Emily's powder first!

"This is a great idea, Billy!" Samantha says when she spots us setting up the buffet. "You're so smart! I bet your dad is amazing! I mean, he has to be. He's *your* dad!"

Manny looks at me and rolls his eyes. I can tell what he's thinking. *You weren't kidding about the fan club!*

As the rest of the kids line up, Principal Gilamon comes out! I didn't know he would be at the fund-raiser. My last school assembly went so terribly . . . what if this fund-raiser heads in the same direction? His presence just adds to the pressure.

Principal Gilamon addresses the people in the cafeteria.

"Students, we have a very special treat for you this evening," he begins. "The dinner at this fund-raiser has been prepared by seventh grader Billy Sure's father, who is a WORLD-CLASS COOK!"

World-class cook? It takes every ounce of restraint on my part not to shoot Emily a glance or simply crack up.

"Mr. Sure, what have you prepared for us today?" asks Principal Gilamon.

"Thank you, Principal Gilamon, for this great honor and opportunity," says Dad. "On the menu today are: tuna and kale casserole, liverwurst stuffed with sausage, lima bean deluxe, a fish and pickle salad, and burgers using artichokes as buns instead of bread. And for dessert . . . chocolate-covered spinach!"

Cries of "Yuck!" "Gross!" and "I want a hot dog!" fill the cafeteria.

"Now, please," Principal Gilamon say, raising his hands to quiet the room. "Let's give Mr. Sure's cooking a chance, shall we?"

One by one, the kids reluctantly fill their plates. From the expressions on their faces, you'd think they were condemned prisoners on their way to eating their last meals.

But then, as kids sample the various concoctions, their complaints start to change to cries of amazement.

"Wow! This is the best thing I've ever tasted!"

"I thought I hated lima beans, but these are as sweet as candy!"

"My mom is a terrible cook. Can you come to my house tonight, Mr. Sure?"

I smile and breathe a huge sigh of relief. Emily's powder really does work on everything! I glance over at Dad standing in the kitchen with his arms folded across his chest and a huge smile on his face.

This has got to make him feel great. And that's the best part of all.

Later that night, Emily, Manny, and I meet up at the office. "I don't know, Billy, we may have to make room at Sure Things, Inc. for another partner," Manny says.

I think the time has come for me to tell Manny about my concerns for the Best Test. Everyone is in a good mood and we obviously have a great new product to market.

"So, Manny, I've been thinking," I begin.

"Uh-oh . . . that could mean trouble," Manny says.

"The fact that I can be good at inventing *and* growing spinach makes me think that the Best Test might actually limit people," I explain. "And Emily is good at pointing out people's flaws *and* also at being an inventor. I'd hate to have our invention narrow or limit people's focus, especially kids, who have the whole world open to them. Now, I know after what happened with the Cat-Dog Translator, the idea of scrapping another invention is not—"

"Scrap it," says Manny. "Emily's powder is without a doubt our Next Big Thing. It's the product that will get us out of our financial hole. Let's get moving on it ASAP."

Emily screams and jumps up and down with joy.

"EMILY'S FOOD POWDER is going to be the biggest Next Big Thing!" she cries.

"Uh . . . no. Not really," says Manny.

"What do you mean?" asks Emily. She looks like she might shoot lasers out of her eyes at Manny. Leave it to Emily to switch moods so quickly.

Manny backs away from Emily. He knows that look. "I just mean that the name could use a little work. Let's keep it simple and direct. Sure Things, Inc.'s Next Big Thing is the GROSS-TO-GOOD POWDER. What do you think?"

"I like it," I say, feeling relieved that Manny was able to let go of the Best Test so easily. "Emily?"

She shrugs. "Whatever. If you're not calling it Emily's Food Powder, then I don't care what you call it. I'm outta here. See ya later."

Manny turns to his desk. "I'm jumping on

the rollout strategy for the Gross-to-Good Powder."

"Great," I say. "I'm exhausted. I'm heading home. See ya tomorrow. And Manny . . . thanks."

"Uh-huh," he says. He's already so lost in product design ideas and marketing schedules, I don't even see him online auctioning.

Right before bed, Mom e-mails me. She got the Best Test prototype in the mail and wants me to video chat with her as she tries it out. I grab Emily so we can video chat with Mom together.

Ping bong bing! Mom's call blares through my speakers. I hit accept, and she appears on-screen.

"It's so great to see you both!" Mom says.

"Miss you, Mom," says Emily.

"Me too," I add. "Are you ready for the test?"

Mom nods. I give her the lock code I programmed on the suitcase just in case it fell into the wrong hands, and out the Best Test comes! She places it on her head. Immediately, the Best Test flashes and rings, then prints out the result.

"Well, this is weird," says Mom, holding the piece of paper to her webcam so Emily and I can read.

I look at the paper.

Carol Sure is best at keeping secrets.

CAROL SURE is Best at Keeping secrets.

"Keeping secrets?" Mom says. "Now that's a laugh! In my book club, everyone knows me as the person who spoils the ending! I'm sorry, honey, but maybe you should work on another invention."

"As a matter of fact," I say. "We have already scrapped the Best Test. After all, it said that Dad was best at cooking."

Mom laughs.

"And Emily is responsible for our Next Big Thing—the Gross-to-Good Powder. Whatever you sprinkle it on tastes great—even Dad's concoctions."

"I slipped some into the saltshaker," Emily admits, "so now Dad's meals tastes great, and we don't ever have to hurt his feelings."

"You should see us ask for seconds, Mom!" I say. "Even Philo! Although he's never been the world's pickiest eater."

"Time to sign off, guys," Mom says. "It's so good to see your faces. I love you both and miss you."

"Love you, Mom," says Emily.

"Good night, Mom," I say. "I love you too."

The screen goes blank and I remember just how much I miss her. And as much as I try to ignore the Best Test's result . . . I can't help but wonder about what it said Mom was best at.

If she's best at keeping secrets, what secret is she keeping from me?

Want more Billy Sure?
Sure you do!
Take a sneak peek at the next
book in the Billy Sure
Kid Entrepreneur series!

"What's the latest on the GROSS-TO-GOOD POWDER?" Emily asks Manny.

Manny continues to tap away on the keyboard.

"Uh, Manny," Emily continues, "when someone asks you a question, the polite thing to do is to answer it. At least that's how it works with NORMAL humans."

Okay, so maybe Emily doesn't want to ship *me* off to Saturn anymore, but I can't say the same for my best friend. . . .

Manny whirls around in his chair to face us.

"Numbers are great. The Midwest is leading the way with a forty-seven percent rise in sales over the last three weeks," he reports.

"See?" I say to Emily.

"I would have thought that our house was leading the way, since we put the powder on every single thing Dad cooks!" Emily jokes.

I love my dad. He's a great artist and gardener, but he is, hands down, the world's worst cook. Dad wasn't always the family chef. My mom travels a lot as a scientist doing research for the government, and about nine months ago she left for her longest trip yet. She wasn't much better at cooking either, but Mom loved to order in pizza. Dad? Well, Dad likes pizza, but with his own additions. Asparagus, kale, codfish, chia seeds, stinky cheese (instead of good cheese) . . . Dad's cooking is really gross.

Only he doesn't think so. Fortunately, Emily filled our saltshaker at home with the Gross-to-Good Powder, so now Dad can keep thinking he's a great cook, we don't have to hurt his feelings by telling him otherwise, and we can stand to eat his cooking every night.

As for my mom, I miss her a lot, although we e-mail all the time and video chat when possible.

And so, at least for the time being, Emily and I have one of Dad's bizarre concoctions to look forward to each night at dinnertime. In fact, Dad is so proud of his cooking that his latest painting project is a series of still lifes based on the strange dishes he's come up with.

It's a little strange. I mean, who would want to buy a painting of jellied tuna?

"That's fantastic, Manny," I say after hearing the rundown of our sales figures.

"Absolutely," replies Manny. Then, without missing a beat, "So, what's next?"

That's my partner. No sooner is one invention on the shelves selling like crazy than Manny is ready to jump onto what we're going to do next.

"I have a file of ideas we've rejected," I say. "Maybe we could rethink one of those." I grab a cardboard file box out from under my desk and pull off the lid. Okay—maybe I'm not the most organized. The file has rejected inventions in it, but it's also got doodles of my favorite baseball team, the Hyenas, and the math homework I forgot to hand in last week.

"Let's see . . . there's the pen that turns into a jet pack . . ." I begin reading off the correct paper. "Nah, getting the engine that small could take years."

"What about another product like the SIBLING SILENCER?" Emily asks. She smiles smugly. Emily loves using Sure Things, Inc.'s second product on me. Last week she silenced me when I was talking about superheroes. Just as I was about to tell her about how I'd love to be invisible, *ZING!* I couldn't talk any more. Note to self: Install a "Billy Immunity" option on future models.

"Actually, I didn't invent that," I say. "That came out of a contest we held where other young inventors submitted their ideas. We picked the one we liked the best and helped the inventor make it a reality."

"So, why not do that again?" asks Emily.

I turn to Manny, who seems to be half-listening and half answering his e-mails, even though he's the one who started this conversation.

"What do you think, Manny?" I ask.

Manny doesn't react. Make that one-quarter listening, and three-quarters answering e-mails.

"I don't think he heard you, Billy," says

Emily. "Working with someone like this every day would drive me—"

"What if we took the contest ONE STEP FURTHER?" Manny says suddenly, turning to look right at us. "What if we made it a TV show?"

Emily shoots me a look that I can only interpret as: Okay, maybe working with this guy is not so bad after all.

"A TV show?" I ask.

"Yeah, where young inventors present everything from rough ideas to preliminary sketches to first-pass prototypes. Then the judges—I'm thinking the three of us—vote. It won't be about who has already made the best invention, but who has the best idea. Just like with the Sibling Silencer, the winning inventor would share in the profits, and the TV show would be marketing in itself!"

"That would be way cooler than just sending your idea to a website," says Emily.

"But how do we even do that?" I ask. "I mean, a TV show? Where do we start?"

"I'll get in touch with Chris Fernell,"

Manny says. "He should be able to point us in the right direction."

Chris Fernell is the host of **Better Than Sleeping!**, the TV show where I was interviewed just after the All Ball hit big. He's somewhat of a friend, or as much of a friend as a TV host can be with a kid, and that's pretty cool.

"This is fantastic," I say. "Doing a TV show again, *and* helping a young inventor, *and* coming up with SURE THINGS' NEXT BIG THING! Wow!"

Looking for another great book?
Find it
IN THE MIDDLE.

Fun, fantastic books for kids in the in-beTWEEN age.

InTheMiddleBooks.com

 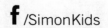